A King Production presents…

The Final Chapter

Who Will Be Left Standing…

JOY DEJA KING

Cover concept by Joy Deja King
Cover Model: Joy Deja King
Editor: Jacqueline Ruiz: tinx518@aol.com

Library of Congress Cataloging-in-Publication Data;
King, Deja Joy
Bitch The Final Chapter: a novel/by Joy Deja King
For complete Library of Congress Copyright info visit;
www.joydejaking.com Twitter: @joydejaking

A King Production
P.O. Box 912, Collierville, TN 38027

A King Production and the above portrayal logo are trademarks of A King Production LLC.

This Book is Dedicated To My:

Family, Readers, and Supporters.
I LOVE you guys so much. Please believe that!!

A special Thank You to Linda Williams, Tracy Taylor,
Rahman Muhammad and Tara Powell aka MissP.
You all have been genuine supporters from #dayone

A special special Thank You to Quinn Villagomez…
Keep "Shimazzing" and Cassandra Carrington for
being a dedicated reader and supporter ☺

Dear Readers:

Can you believe this is it!! The first installment of the Bitch Series...Bitch The Beginning dropped in 2006. That was 10 years ago. It brings tears to my eyes that this Series has lasted so long. But whoever follows my books, you know it ain't REALLY over!! LOL!! Yes, this is the last book in the Bitch Series but as long as I have breath in my body, these characters will live on. They're like my family and I love them...flaws and all ☺ I do hope you all enjoy this final installment and I LOVE and appreciate each and every one of you that has remained loyal and supported my work. This is for you!!

Love Always,

Joy Deja King

A KING PRODUCTION

Bitch

The Final Chapter

Who Will Be Left Standing...

JOY DEJA KING

"Karma's Such A Thing Of Beauty..."

Drake

Chapter One

No Redemption

"Keep that gun to his motherfuckin' head. If that nigga sneeze, you pull the trigger," Supreme directed his henchman, Trigger, eyeing Arnez as he pressed down on the gas pedal headed towards Brooklyn.

"Supreme, man I got you. It don't have to be like this. You the winner in this game. No need for the threats." Even in his current predicament, Arnez believed he could plead his way out of a death sentence.

"This ain't no game. That's yo' first mistake thinking that it is."

"I didn't mean it like that, Supreme. No disrespect. All I'm sayin'—"

"I don't wanna hear shit you saying," Supreme barked, cutting Arnez off. "Unless you giving me directions to where you have my daughter stashed."

"I got you. I'm taking you there now."

"You better be, but more importantly, Aaliyah better be alive," Supreme made clear before reaching over and pressing the tip of the gun to Arnez's head. "If she's not, you might as well stop breathing now 'cause you already dead," he warned before focusing his eyes back on the dark road.

"Your daughter's safe... you have my word on that, Supreme." As confident as Arnez sounded with his statement, deep down he knew it was a roll of the dice whether Aaliyah was dead or alive. Her fate relied solely on Maya's crazy ass and that made Arnez uneasy to say the least. Not only was he uneasy he was pissed the fuck off. Because not only was Aaliyah's life in Maya's hands, so was his.

I should've known not to fuck wit' yo' trifling ass, Maya. Now you got me all jammed up on some bullshit you orchestrated. I already had to watch Supreme kill Emory 'cause of your fucked up antics and there's a good chance I'm next. I swear, if I somehow manage to stay alive tonight, you don't have to worry about Supreme killing you 'cause that ass is mine, Arnez thought to himself as fear began to sink in.

"Please let Aaliyah be alive," Arnez mumbled under his breath as Supreme pulled in front of the nondescript house that Aaliyah had been held up in for the last few months.

"My dad still isn't answering his phone," Xavier complained to his grandfather, pacing the floor back and forth. He continued to call his father nonstop, determined to get him to answer.

"Son, relax," Quentin said, patting Xavier on the shoulder. He hated seeing his grandson all worked up, especially knowing it was because of his own daughter, Maya.

"I don't know how you can be so calm."

"It's called old age." Quentin chuckled. "You have to always try and remain calm even under the most strenuous circumstances," he explained.

Quentin was doing his best to mask his fear in front of Xavier because he didn't want his grandson to worry, but his heart and conscience were in disarray. The very idea that Maya could be responsible for any harm being done to Aaliyah and Precious made Quentin physically ill.

"Grandfather, are you okay?" Xavier questioned, noticing Quentin sitting down in the chair as if in pain.

"I'm fine," he said reaching for the glass of water on the coffee table.

"You don't look fine. Did you take your medicine?" Xavier was well aware that his grandfather was still being treated by his physician from when he was shot a few years ago. Due to his age and the injuries he sustained, he was on a strict pill regimen.

"I'm okay. I took my medicine on an empty stomach and it made me a little light headed," Quentin lied. He was light headed, but it had nothing to do with his medicine. Quentin's guilt over Maya had him on the verge of having a nervous breakdown.

"Open the fuckin' door," Supreme ordered Arnez. He seemed to be fidgeting to retrieve the key as if stalling. "What the fuck is takin' you so long! Don't act like you ain't got the key," Supreme barked.

"Nah, nah, I got it. But, umm, feeling the coldness of that metal on the side of my head is making a nigga anxious." Arnez gave a nervous laugh as he put the key in the doorknob. His heart was racing as visions of what was on the other side of the door were flashing through his mind.

Please don't let this girl be dead. If she is, all my plans are about to blow up in smoke because that crazy bitch Maya couldn't keep her trigger happy ass in check, Arnez thought shaking his head.

"Move out the way!" Supreme shouted, flinging

open the door, almost knocking Arnez down as he made his way inside.

"What in the hell happened in here," Arnez uttered, unable to contain his disbelief at what they had walked in on.

Supreme rushed through the basement apartment trying to find any evidence that Aaliyah and Precious were okay. Instead all he got was more unanswered questions and a strong indication that his daughter and ex-wife didn't make it out of this hell-hole alive.

"There's so much blood," Supreme mumbled, looking around the small room. He glanced at the broken lamp, trash all over the floor from the garbage can being knocked over, and then he noticed a glimmer of gold. It was halfway hidden underneath an area rug. Supreme leaned forward to get a better look. He closed his eyes and shook his head.

"This belongs to Aaliyah." Supreme sighed, kneeling down to pick up the gold nameplate necklace that had her name emblazoned in diamonds. Supreme had given it to her when Aaliyah was sixteen and she never took it off. Now he was holding what was a cherished possession of his daughter's and there were several drops of blood, more than likely hers, on it. "My poor baby girl," he kept repeating as a single tear escaped his eye.

Supreme felt as if the walls were closing in on him. With so much blood and no trace of Aaliyah or Precious, he had to come to the realization that his daughter and the love of his life might be dead.

"Damn I'm sorry," Trigger huffed, witnessing how distraught his boss was.

"I'ma take great pleasure in killing yo' moth-erfuckin' ass," Supreme stood and roared; ready to rip off Arnez's neck with his bare hands. "Where the fuck that nigga at!" Supreme shouted.

Trigger turned around and realized Arnez was gone. "Boss, I only stepped away for a quick minute to see what you had bent down to look at. I had my eyes off of him for a second." Supreme was already halfway out the door by the time Trigger finished pleading his case. He ran after Supreme with both his guns aimed to kill, but Arnez was long gone.

Chapter Two

911

Maya was bent over in pain as she pressed down on the bullet wound she had sustained from her shoot out with Precious. The blood was steadily flowing and Maya knew she needed medical attention ASAP.

"Fuck!" she screamed out while wrapping a t-shirt she retrieved from a bag of clothes in her trunk around her stomach. "I can't believe that bitch Precious shot me, but that's okay. I got the best of her and her dumbass daughter," Maya boasted out loud, trying to find the silver lining in her fucked up predicament.

No matter how she flipped it though, Maya was in bad shape. Her white t-shirt was now fire engine red. Without a second thought her finger went to dial her father Quentin. Maya was so used to pulling the wool over her father's eyes, having him believe whatever lies and fairytales she sold him that it was second nature for her to believe he would save the day once again. But then reality quickly crept in.

If I call my father he's gonna drill the fuck outta me. How will I be able to explain all this blood? Fuck calling him. I don't need that headache right now. Emory will have to do, Maya thought to herself before hitting the call button.

"Answer the fuckin' phone!" Maya yelled into the phone when it kept ringing then went to voicemail. "This stupid motherfucker would not answer the phone when I need his dumbass," Maya screamed. She was about to blow Emory's phone up nonstop, but then she saw him calling her back. "Why the fuck didn't you answer when I called you?" Maya popped.

"Calm down my love. Don't get yourself all worked up."

"Who is this?" Maya questioned, looking at the phone as if maybe she had dialed the wrong number and now the person was calling her back.

"Come on now. As much history as we share. You don't recognize my voice. You've hurt my feelings."

Maya's eyes widened in disbelief. She recognized the voice on the other end of the phone. She was starting to wish she had followed her first instinct and called her father instead, but Maya wasn't

willing to fold her hand just yet.

"Hello... are you still there?" Arnez said in an almost singing tone. Maya felt as if maybe he was taunting her.

"I'm here. Arnez, I'm so happy to hear your voice!"

"If you wanted to hear my voice, why didn't you dial my number instead of Emory's?"

"I tried calling your number, but for some reason I wasn't able to get through. Emory told me he was meeting you so I called him instead."

"My phone seems to be working just fine. I have been trying to get myself out a bit of a jam. Maybe that's why we couldn't connect." Arnez chuckled. "I had no idea you were friends with Emory."

"We aren't exactly friends. I recently met him through one of my connects and I was considering doing some business with him," Maya mumbled trying to disguise how much pain she was in. She was sick of the bullshit small talk with Arnez, but she wanted to see how much he knew and also figure out why in the hell he had Emory's phone.

"I see."

"Yes, he mentioned he was cool with you, but with so much going on I haven't had the chance to mention it to you. So why are you answering Emory's phone?"

"He's sorta unavailable at the moment."

"Unavailable?" There was no denying the confusion in Maya's voice, but she pressed forward. "So when will Emory be available?

"Not sure, but is there something I can assist you with?"

Between Arnez's voice sounding as if he genuinely wanted to help and Maya being desperate for medical attention she rolled the dice and hoped for the best.

"I've been shot. I'm losing a lot of blood. I need to get to a doctor before I pass out," Maya finally admitted, feeling like her body was being drained of all energy.

"Lucky for you, I can help with that, but it's gonna cost you," Arnez revealed. Maya could practically see Arnez grinning through the phone. But in her current predicament she was willing to agree to just about anything. Maya wasn't ready to die and if making a fucked up deal with Arnez would save her life, then she was all in.

"This shit right here bumpin'," Nekesa, said to her homegirl Adama as they drove down the street listening to Drake's new mixtape. They had the windows rolled all the way down and the volume all the way up, trying to find some trouble to get into.

"Play that shit again. That might be my favorite song right there." Adama smiled, nodding her head to the beat.

"That song is fire," Nekesa agreed, turning her

head all the way around. She then took her hands off the steering wheel to do a dance she saw some chicks doing in a youtube video.

"Girl you crazy!" Adama laughed, cheering her friend on. They then started doing the hand motions to the dance in unison as if they were in the club. It wasn't until they heard the loud continuous honking of a horn and bright high beams being flashed that they stepped out of their imaginary club performance.

"Fuck!!!!!!!" both girls wailed upon realizing their car had swerved to the other lane and was about to cause a head-on collision. Luckily the shock of knocking on death's door didn't cause Nekesa to have a complete meltdown. Instead she used those same hands she was dancing with a second ago to maneuver the steering wheel off the road, barely missing the front bumper of the other car.

The besties weren't completely in the clear. The accelerated speed Nekesa used to not crash into the other car caused her to hit something else on the dim lit street. The girls' bodies jilted forward then backwards as Nekesa pressed down firmly on the brakes.

"Are we alive?" Adama asked not opening her eyes.

"I heard that dumbass question you just asked so that's a good sign." Nekesa sighed unbuckling her seat belt.

"My question wasn't dumb. I really thought we were about to die," Adama huffed.

"I ain't even gonna lie. I was scared as shit too. But now that I know we're okay, I'm scared for another reason."

"Why?'

"To see the damage to my mom's car. She gon' kill me! What the fuck did I hit?" Nekesa said, getting out the car.

"Yeah, it definitely doesn't help that you stole it."

"I didn't steal it. I took it without her permission. There's a difference," Nekesa tried to clarify. "Oh shit! The entire front grill is fucked up! This car accident didn't put me in the hospital, but moms damn sure is," Nekesa said shaking her head damn near in tears. I can't believe this fire hydrant did all this damage."

"OMG!" Adama cried, then covered her mouth in horror.

"What's wrong?!" Nekesa wanted to know before she started panicking.

"You need to call 911!"

"I know the car looked fucked up, but it ain't that bad! I can still get us home," Nekesa argued, annoyed by what she considered Adama being overly dramatic.

"You hit more than a fire hydrant," Adama said shaking her head. There are two women on the side of the road and I think they're dead."

When Nekesa walked around to the side of the car where Adama was standing, her heart felt like it dropped to her stomach. Both girls burst out crying until they finally worked up enough nerves to call the police.

Chapter Three

Complicated

"Are you sure you heard Arnez correctly?" Nico questioned, not convinced with the validity of what Genesis was telling him.

"Yes!" Genesis growled in frustration, knocking over some papers on his desk. "I know what I heard Arnez say. He told me I had a choice to either save my wife and the mother of my child or my new love. I've only married one woman and she is the mother of my child. That woman is Talisa," Genesis said getting choked up. He had buried the pain he endured from losing her on their wedding day for so long that bringing it back to the surface had him caught up in his feelings.

"Listen, maybe I'm expressing myself wrong. What I mean is, Arnez is a sick psychopath. You have been in his line of destruction for years. He would do or say anything to rile you up. Even lie about your wife being alive. That isn't even possible... I mean you saw her dead body... right?"

"Yes... but not really," Genesis said feeling overwhelmed with confusion. "That day is such a blur to me. The love of my life, the woman I exchanged vows with and planned to spend the rest of my life with, died in my arms or so I thought. Then when we got to the hospital an emergency c-section had to be done to save my son's life so he wouldn't die too. So yes, I did see Talisa, but it was brief," Genesis admitted putting his head down as he relived what he considered to be the worst day of his life.

"What about the funeral?"

"I showed up, but mentally I had checked out. I let her parents make all the arrangements. They blamed me for her death and the guilt was eating me up alive. I wasn't in the right mind to handle any of that. I believed that was Talisa in the casket, but I don't know anymore. I just don't know."

"Genesis, don't let Arnez take you down this dark path. Talisa is dead."

"But what if she isn't? There was something about the tone in his voice that made me believe

Arnez was telling the truth. As crazy as it sounds, what if my wife is truly alive?"

"So, Talisa how did you end up here?" Skylar inquired as the two women sat on the beach eating the fresh fruit they were given that morning.

"It's a long complicated story so I'll give you the short version. On my wedding day, after I had exchanged vows with my husband, my ex-boyfriend shot me. I always thought he wanted me dead, but I was wrong since he's the one that kidnapped me and had me brought to this island."

"Your ex is responsible for this? That means he must be responsible for me being here too. But why would your ex kidnap me?" Skylar was baffled.

"Do you know a man by the name of Arnez?"

Why does that name sound so familiar to me, Skylar thought to herself.

"Or what about Genesis?" Talisa asked casually as she bit down on a mango.

Skylar's head began to spin when she heard the name Genesis. She was smart enough to know that there is such a thing as a small world, but it ain't that small. The pieces to the puzzle began shifting around in her mind. The island beauty sitting in front of her with the glistening brown skin and angelic smile wasn't some random Talisa it was 'THE' Talisa, who was supposed to be the dead wife of her man.

"Neither name sounds familiar. I don't know Arnez or Genesis," Skylar lied as she nibbled on a strawberry. "So I'm assuming your ex is Arnez?"

"Yes, that's correct."

"So who is Genesis?' Skylar wanted confirmation for what she already knew.

"Genesis is my husband and the love of my life. We have a son together. I still want to break down and cry when I think about not seeing my baby grow up. I've missed every milestone in his life."

Skylar immediately feared that that would become her fate. Not seeing her own son grow up sent chills down her spine. "There has to be a way off this island," she uttered.

"I haven't been able to find it." Talisa shrugged. "Arnez constantly has guards watching me around the clock. The crazy part is they're actually very nice. Especially the women that cook and take care of me. Besides them not speaking English all that well, they try to make sure all my needs are met."

"Do you ever see Arnez?"

"He visits the island once a month. I guess to check to make sure everything is running smoothly. But Arnez hasn't been here the last couple months," Talisa said gazing at the calm waves in the ice blue water. "Now that I think about it, that's rather strange. I wonder what's keeping him away, although I don't mind. Every time I see his face, it's like reliving my

worse nightmare over and over again. Part of me has even given up on ever escaping."

"I'm not giving up!" Skylar said with the quickness. "I will get back to my son and my man. I don't care what I have to do."

"Maybe that's the reason you were brought here. To light that fire back inside of me so I would fight to get back home to my family. Lately it's been fading away. I was tired of being disappointed over and over again. The little glimmer that was left seemed to be burning out. But you're giving me hope. If we work together we can both get back to our loved ones."

"Yes, maybe we can." Skylar smiled reluctantly. Her heart did break for Talisa, knowing that for all these years she had been kept away from her husband and child. But ultimately, her loyalty was to her own heart. Genesis was the man of Skylar's dreams and she was not about to let him reunite with his presumed dead wife if it meant she had to let him go. For now, Skylar decided to put her concerns about the lovebirds ever reuniting on the backburner. Her mission was to find a way off the island and to accomplish that she would need Talisa's help. So Skylar would do what was necessary to keep the distressed damsel on her side. Which meant not disclosing that they were both trying to get home to the same man.

Chapter Four

Moment Of Truth

"Supreme, I have other business to take care of so I'ma need you to get right to the point. I think we can all agree that no one in this room has time to waste," Nico scoffed. He made eye contact with Genesis, Quentin, Amir, and even Lorenzo, making sure each man was on his side.

"I know there is no love lost between us, Nico, but I don't believe in wasting time, especially my own. If I told each of you to be here then it's for good reason."

"Which is?" Lorenzo questioned.

"It's regarding Precious and Aaliyah."

"What about them?" they all asked simultaneously.

"There's no easy way to say this, but there's a good chance they're dead."

All the air seemed to disperse from the room. Quentin reached for his chest as if about to have a heart attack. He felt in his coat pocket for his medicine and quickly swallowed two pills without any water. He needed to get his blood pressure down now not later.

"Are you sure, Supreme?" Amir's question was direct without emotion. He wasn't ready to mourn for Aaliyah. Not now, not ever.

"No, I'm not sure, but..."

"Then why you bring us all together to tell us this shit then!" Nico exploded. "Keep that shit to yo'self until you got some motherfuckin' proof!" Nico continued.

"Nico, calm down." Genesis put his hand on Nico's shoulder trying to deescalate his rage.

"Don't fuckin' tell me to calm down!" he barked, jerking his shoulder away from Genesis. "You come in here gettin' everybody riled up and you ain't got no proof. Get the fuck outta here wit' that. My daughter ain't dead and neither is my wi..." Nico caught himself before saying the word wife. Yes, he and Precious were still married, but on paper only. "Precious isn't dead either," he then said putting his hand over his mouth.

"Aaliyah is my daughter too and..."

"No!" Nico roared cutting Supreme off before he could finish his sentence. "Aaliyah is *my* daughter," he stressed. "My blood runs through her body, not yours. It's time you accept that."

The vein in Supreme's neck seemed to dilate and then throb. His fury over what Nico said was evident. Everyone knew he was about to go nuclear at any moment.

"I understand you're lashing out at me 'cause you hurt right now," Supreme said biting down on his lip, doing his best to keep his temper in check. "But everyone in this room loves Precious and Aaliyah so we all hurtin'. Let's put our energy into finding out what happened to them and not do this," Supreme reasoned.

"I know what happened," Amir stepped forward and said. "It was Maya. Maya is the reason Aaliyah and Precious are dead."

"Stop saying that shit! We don't know if they're dead," Nico insisted.

"Nico, you're right," Supreme conceded. "We don't know if they're dead. What I do know is I went to the location where Aaliyah had been held. Clearly there had been a struggle, there was blood everywhere and I found the necklace I gave Aaliyah years go."

"Dear God." Quentin gasped, covering his face with his hand.

"No... no... no," Nico mumbled, taking small

steps back and forth.

"This can't be happening," Lorenzo stated under his breath, walking over to Genesis. "Do you really think they're dead?" Lorenzo asked Genesis after pulling him over to the side for some privacy.

"It's not looking good," Genesis hated to admit. "First Angel, now Aaliyah and Precious. I don't know how much more Nico can take."

"Angel... who is Angel?" Lorenzo wanted to know.

"Damn, I didn't mean for that to slip out."

"Genesis, you can tell me. What's going on?"

"Angel is Nico's daughter."

"I didn't know Nico had another daughter," Lorenzo said surprised by the information.

"Neither did he. He only recently found out. By the time Nico did the young lady went missing and he hasn't been able to locate her."

"Wow, is she younger or older than Aaliyah?"

"A few years younger. Nico hasn't told anybody but me. So you..."

"I know. Have to keep it to myself," Lorenzo said, finishing the sentence for Genesis. "You don't have to worry about me saying anything. Now I see why Nico exploded on Supreme. He's gettin' it from every direction."

"Exactly. Surprisingly, Supreme handled it very well. I just knew blows were about to be exchanged."

"It's probably because Supreme understands Nico's pain better than anyone else. They may not like each other, but the one thing they do share is their long history and deep love for Precious and they both adore Aaliyah," Lorenzo said.

"You're right. I know this can't be easy for you either," Genesis added.

"It's not. There was a time I thought Precious and I might get married one day. But then I found out Dior was alive and she came back in my life. And Precious realized that Supreme was still the love of her life. It worked out for me, I was hoping it would work out for her too."

"So was I... so was I..." Genesis repeated as his voice trailed off with disappointment.

"Listen," Supreme stated loudly wanting to get everyone's attention. "I know I said there was a very good chance that Aaliyah and Precious aren't alive, but that doesn't mean I'm giving up. I have my men searching everywhere for them. Whether they are dead or alive, I will bring them home."

"What about Maya? When will we find her dead body? It's time for her reign of destruction to come to an end," Amir said.

"Slow down, Amir. We don't know for sure Maya is responsible," Quentin said, trying to come to his daughter's defense.

"No disrespect, Quentin, but wake up! Does Maya need to put a bullet through your head for you to see she's nothing but a psychotic killer?"

"Amir, that's enough," Genesis said, giving his son a stern glare.

"Amir is right," Supreme chimed in. "Maya is the one responsible for what happened. She was playing both Arnez and Emory. Behind the scenes pulling all the strings."

"Arnez... so Maya was working with Arnez?" Genesis wanted to confirm.

"Yes, she was. Arnez was the one who took me to the location in Brooklyn where Aaliyah was being held."

"Where is Arnez now?" Genesis had his own unfinished business to handle with Arnez.

"Unfortunately, I'm not sure. He managed to get away before I could take him out."

"Supreme if you find Arnez before me, I ask that you not kill him."

"Why would I do that? Even if he didn't pull the trigger, he's just as responsible for what happened to Aaliyah and Precious as Maya is."

"So is Emory if he was working with Maya," Amir added.

"I've already handled Emory and Arnez is next."

"Supreme, please. Arnez is responsible for the kidnaping of Skylar and possibly my wife."

All eyes shifted on Genesis. His last statement puzzled them.

"Dad, my mother is dead. Why would you think Arnez had her kidnapped?"

"Amir, I'll discuss the details with you later. The point is, I need Arnez alive. At least until I can find out where Sklyar is and find out the truth about Talisa. Can you please do that for me, Supreme?"

"If I find Arnez before you, I won't kill him until you get what you need," Supreme agreed grudgingly. "Now if you all will excuse me. I need to go speak to my son."

"Please keep me in the loop," Quentin yelled out as Supreme was walking out the door.

"Why so you can try to save Maya's worthless life by warning her about what's going on?" Amir stated angrily.

"Amir, I told you that's enough!" Genesis shouted.

"You're right. I've had enough! Maybe if you weren't so concerned about protecting Quentin and had killed Maya when we had the chance, Aaliyah and Precious would still be alive! I'm done here," Amir scoffed before storming out.

"Amir, get back here!" Genesis yelled, but all he heard was the door slam after Amir walked out. "I apologize for my son's behavior, Quentin. You know how close he was to Aaliyah."

"You don't owe me an apology. If anything I owe Amir and everyone else in this room an apology. Precious begged me to see the truth about Maya and I refused. A part of me still doesn't want to believe that she's responsible for all the hell this family has been going though." Quentin shook his head.

"Quentin, if you want to save Maya, you better find her first. Because if I get my hands on her before you do... you'll be burying two daughters." Nico's words stung Quentin to the core and for the first time left the patriarch of the family speechless.

Chapter Five

Zero Loyalty

"I can't believe I hit two people with my car," Nekesa cried nervously, biting down on her nails. She and Adama sat at the police station waiting to be interviewed. They both wondered how a night of fun turned into a scene from a horror film.

"Are you sure you don't want to call your mom?" Adama asked, fidgeting with hands.

"No! I'm already in enough trouble. I can't take hearing my mom's mouth right now. Maybe you should call your dad. He's always pretty cool about things," Nekesa suggested.

"My dad's out of town and you already know I can't call my mother."

"Well you girl's better call somebody," Detective Garcia walked in and said. Both girls looked up at the funny built Hispanic man in the cheap suit with tears in their eyes.

"Detective, I'm so sorry," Nekesa stood up and said. "Are they going to be okay?"

"You young ladies might be looking at murder charges. Now I'll read your Miranda rights before I continue.

"Murder!" Nekesa and Adama both blurted out. "They're dead!" they screamed.

"It was an accident! I didn't mean to hit them with my car! I swear it was an accident!" Nekesa stood up and pleaded.

"You did more then hit them with your car. One or both of you," Detective Garcia said, staring down at Nekesa and Adama with accusing eyes, "shot those women. You can make this easy or hard for yourself. Now do either one of you care to tell me where the murder weapon is? I'm waiting...."

"The doctor said he got you healed up nicely and all you need is a little rest and you'll be okay." Arnez smiled, sitting down next to Maya.

"Yeah, he saved my life. Thank you. I'm sure he cost you a pretty penny."

"I'm not worried about that since it's coming out your pocket." Arnez chuckled. "I'm sure you didn't expect me to pay for it."

"Of course I didn't," Maya snapped turning away. "Why would I think you'd ever do anything to help me just because," she said sarcastically. "I guess that would be asking too much. Especially given we're supposed to be partners and lovers." Maya gave a slight pout like she felt betrayed and hurt by Arnez.

"Cut the bullshit, Maya!" Arnez used his elbow to press down on the bullet injury the doctor just finished patching up less than thirty minutes ago.

The pain was so excruciating that Maya couldn't even scream out. Her face simply froze in a death frown. No words escaped her mouth. She was at Arnez's mercy.

"You sent Emory to kill me. You deceitful lowdown bitch. You have zero loyalty. I should break your neck right now, but I still need you alive," Arnez scoffed, pressing down even harder on Maya's injury. "But if you don't do exactly as I say, you're going to wish I broke your neck. Why? Because I'm going to personally deliver you to Supreme and let him kill you." Arnez began laughing uncontrollably. "I can only imagine the torture he'll put you through after you murdered his daughter and beloved Precious." His eyes danced with pleasure at the very thought. "So do we understand each other?" Arnez continued to taunt Maya and pressed down even harder one last time before releasing his elbow.

"Aaaaaaaaaaahhhhh...." Maya hollered out in pain and relief now that Arnez was off her. "You sick bastard!"

"It only makes sense that one sick person would recognize another."

"Whatever." Maya shrugged, shaking her head. "I knew Emory wouldn't be able to finish the job. I should've done it myself," Maya mumbled under her breath. Lucky for her, Arnez didn't hear the last part of her sentence.

"Emory was very close to getting the job done, actually."

"So what happened?"

"Supreme showed up and saved the day. That's also when Emory filled us in on his relationship with you and how you lied and said I had killed Aaliyah. Since I knew where Aaliyah was being held, Supreme found me more useful so Emory had to go."

"Supreme killed Emory?" she sounded stunned. Maya was well aware that Supreme was capable of murder, but she never thought he would be the one to take out Emory.

"He sure did!" Arnez had this proud grin on his face that had Maya seething. "After so many years of being a superstar Supreme still hasn't lost it. You would think after living in all those multi-million dollar houses, driving expensive cars and private jets he would've lost his edge. But nope, he's just as cutthroat... maybe even more so." Arnez winked.

"I see you're a Supreme dick rider like everyone else." Maya rolled her eyes and looked around for her pain pills. She needed something to knock her out so she wouldn't have to lay there and listen to the sound of Arnez's voice or see his face.

"I'm no dick rider, but I'll admit I have a lot of respect for Supreme. There are very few men that reach his level of success who stay grounded and remain true to themselves. Even after all the bullshit that woman put him through."

"Who, Precious?" Maya asked.

"What other woman has he ever loved... of course I'm talking about Precious. But even after everything they've been through, he would still lie, kill and risk his life for her. Hell, Aaliyah ain't even really his daughter, but he'll put a bullet through your head if he ever heard you say otherwise. I can't help but respect him, 'cause it couldn't be me."

"Enough already!" Maya's blood was boiling listening to Arnez go on about Supreme's love for Precious and Aaliyah. She never forgot about the brief fling they shared many years ago and even secretly hoped that maybe one day they could rekindle it. Maya knew that would be next to impossible but a girl can dream.

"I must've struck a nerve... oh yes." Arnez nodded his head. "How can I forget? You had your own infatuation with Supreme. Don't tell me you're still carrying a torch for him," Arnez joked.

Maya's face turned red from anger and embarrassment. "Just shut up!"

Arnez raised his eyebrow and studied Maya's facial expression carefully. "Hold up, you're even crazier than I thought. You really thought there might still be a chance for you and Supreme?" Arnez then let out a loud, obnoxious chuckle.

"Can you please leave? I have to take my medicine and get some rest. If you need my help then first I need to get better."

"Point taken. I'll leave you to recuperate because the moment you do, I'm putting you to work."

Maya gave Arnez a sinister smirk and watched as he left the room. "I hate that sonofabitch!" Maya pounded her fist down on the bed after the door closed.

Arnez thinks he's won and holds my life in his hands. He's gonna be in for a rude awakening. Once I get my strength back, the first life I'm plotting on taken is his. Then I'll have to figure out how to get myself out of this mess. I'm sure Supreme has told anyone that will listen including my father that I'm behind everything including Aaliyah's kidnapping. But with Emory, Aaliyah, and Precious all dead the only weak link left is Arnez. After I kill him, there will be no one left to dispute my version of what really happened. So that means I'll be winning. Maya smiled to herself before closing her eyes and going to sleep to get some much needed rest.

Chapter Six

Don't Wake Me...
I'm Dreaming

"Where am I... somebody please tell me where I am..."

"Get the doctor... now!" one of the nurses called out. "Tell him she's awake."

"Who are you?" Aaliyah asked. Everything was blurry from being heavily medicated. She couldn't get a clear vision of who was in front of her.

"My name is Amy. I'm your nurse. You're in the ICU. You've been here for a couple weeks."

"ICU... what happened to me?" Aaliyah slurred her words as she tried to rise up out the hospital bed. She quickly fell back down due to being physically weak.

"You don't remember what..." the nurse stopped mid sentence when she heard someone come in.

"How is she?" the doctor walked over to Aaliyah and began examining her.

"She's out of it. Most of that has to do with the medicine of course.

"Miss, can you open your eyes?" the doctor questioned but got no response. That quickly Aaliyah had fallen back into a deep sleep. "While the patient was awake did she tell you her name?"

"I didn't have a chance to ask. When she opened her eyes she asked me where she was and what happened."

"Call Detective Garcia and let him know that one of the patients woke up."

"But we still don't know her name or the other woman that was brought in with her. That's not going to help his investigation."

"Amy, just make the call. I told the detective we would be in touch if there were any updates. The patient opening her eyes and speaking is an update. Find me immediately if she wakes up again. Now excuse me, I have other patients to see."

Amy watched as the doctor left the room before glancing back over at a sleeping Aaliyah. She took out her cell phone but instead of doing as she was told and calling Detective Garcia, Amy placed another call first.

"I told you not to call me unless it was important."

"Then clearly it's important," Amy shot back.

"What is it?"

"Aaliyah woke up."

"When?

"A few minutes ago, but she fell right back to sleep. The extra dosage of medicine I've been pumping in her system is keeping her pretty much out of it."

"What about Precious?"

"No. She's still in a coma. It's not looking good for her at all," Amy revealed.

"Did Aaliyah say anything about what happened when she woke up?"

"Nope. Surprisingly she asked me what happened and where she was. Not sure if the drugs I've been giving her is messing with her memory. By the time the doctor came in to question her she was out of it."

"This all sounds promising."

"Before you start rejoicing. The reason I'm calling is because the doctor wants me to call the detective that's working the case. I'm positive he'll want to come to the hospital and see Aaliyah for himself. I would hate for her to wake up while he's here."

"Then go ahead and kill her. That way the nosey detective won't ever be able to speak to her."

"I already told you, it's too risky for me to kill her. If she dies on my watch, that hard-nosed doctor will demand an investigation. When it points back to me, I'll spend the rest of my life in prison. You're not paying me enough to commit murder."

"Name your price."

"There isn't one."

"Then I guess I'll have to do it myself."

"Good luck, but you better work fast because I can't stall much longer. If I don't call that detective, the doctor will become suspicious. I can't raise any red flags. But I did want to give you a heads up to what's going on so you can make your move."

"Thanks, Amy. How much time do I have?"

"The doctor is scheduled to perform surgery in 30 minutes. I would say you have about three hours to handle your business."

"It will be tight, but it's doable. I'll be—"

"Say no more," Amy said cutting the person she was speaking to off. "I don't want to hear the details about what you plan to do. Just do it and leave me out of it. I'm giving you three hours starting now," she said abruptly ending the phone call.

Quentin was on the balcony of his high-rise condo, smoking a cigar when he realized that he had missed two calls from a private number. Initially he disregarded the calls until a few minutes later he noticed his phone ringing again.

"Hello," he answered cautiously, wondering who could be calling him multiple times from a private number. There was a brief moment of eerie silence before the person on the other end finally spoke up.

"Daddy, it's me."

"Maya," Quentin whispered, closing the glass door so Amir couldn't hear him. "Where are you and what have you done to Precious and Aaliyah?" he asked with disdain in his voice.

"Daddy, I haven't done anything... I swear. I've been set up," Maya said in her best tear-filled voice.

"That's not what I've heard. Set up by who?" he asked not sounding convinced.

"Arnez. This is all his doing. I realized that he had been lying to me and was holding Aaliyah hostage. When I threatened to go to the police unless he let Aaliyah go he tried to kill me," Maya cried.

"Where are you? I'll come get you."

"Daddy, can you hear me! Daddy!"

"I'm here, Maya. I can hear you. Can you hear me?"

"Daddy... Daddy..." Maya kept calling out as if she was unable to hear what her father was saying. "Daddy, I think we have a bad connection... Daddy heeeeeeelp me..." Maya's voice trailed off before she ended the call.

"Maya! Maya! Maya!" Quentin kept yelling becoming alarmed. He then looked down at his phone and realized their call had been disconnected. "Damn!" Quentin barked. He then tried to call Maya on her cell phone, but it went straight to voicemail.

"Grandfather, is everything alright?" Xavier opened the glass door and asked. "I heard you out here yelling."

"Sorry about that, son. I was on a business call and things got a little heated," he lied.

"You know the doctor said you have to take it easy. Getting yourself worked up isn't good for your condition."

"You're right. I'll take it easy," Quentin said sitting down.

"Good. I don't want anything happening to you. I'm already worried about my mother and sister. I don't wanna have to worry about you too."

"I know, son. You're dealing with a lot right now."

"We all are. I've never seen my dad so stressed before. He's usually always so calm and in control. But lately he's so on edge. I think he's gonna snap any moment."

"I've known your father for many years. Supreme has had everything you can imagine thrown at him, but yet that man is still standing. I know this Precious and Aaliyah situation is killing him softly, but he'll survive, if only to be strong for you. That's the type of man he is."

"I'm sure you're right, but I don't need him to be strong for me. He's done that all my life. I want to step up and be strong for him and the rest of the family. I feel like I should be doing more." Xavier shook his head in frustration.

"There's nothing you or anyone else can do right now but wait. You need to be focusing on school and going off to college in a couple months."

"Grandfather, I'm not thinking about college right now! All I care about is finding my mother and sister and getting my hands on Maya. 'Cause she gotta go!" Xavier spit in a ruthless tone that stunned Quentin. He had never heard his grandson speak in that manner.

"Before you crucify Maya let's hear what she has to say. Things aren't always what they seem."

"Grandfather, I understand that's your daughter but come on. The writing is on the wall. My dad told me how Maya manipulated this situation."

"I know your father means well. But he is basing his opinion on what Arnez, a known criminal and killer said. That man can't be trusted."

Xavier rolled his eyes before resting his chin on both fists. He let out a heavy sigh, standing up. "My father warned me that you would be defending Maya because you didn't want to see the truth. I was hoping he was wrong, but I guess not."

"Xavier, wait! Don't walk off, son," Quentin implored. "Your father is right. I am guilty of constantly defending Maya. But she's my daughter and I love her. One day when you become a parent you'll understand."

"I'll never understand you defending a monster like Maya. She's not your only daughter, you know. So is my mother and let's not forget your granddaughter."

"I could never forget Precious or Aaliyah. I would gladly give my life for them. Maya may very well be behind all this madness, but there is also a very good chance that's she a victim too. All I'm asking is that you keep an open mind until we get all the facts. Can you do that for me?" Quentin and Xavier locked eyes and held them on each other for an extended period of time before Xavier spoke up.

"I can do that."

"Thank you, son." Quentin smiled.

"Don't thank me yet, Grandfather. When all the facts come out, if it's confirmed that Maya was the mastermind behind everything, I'll be standing in line right behind my father to take Maya out once and for all," Xavier promised.

Chapter Seven

Intruder

The hallways in the ICU were seemingly silent as the nurses were changing shifts just as Amy told her it would be. It gave the unidentified woman a perfect opportunity to sneak into Aaliyah's room without being noticed. She looked around to make sure the few people in the vicinity weren't paying attention although she was dressed in nurse attire and her face was covered. The woman virtually blended in as she eased her way into the door and closed it behind her.

Aaliyah was sleeping peacefully, completely unaware that death had once again come knocking.

"I'll try to make this as peaceful as possible," the woman whispered all the while smiling at the idea of Aaliyah being dead in a matter of minutes. She gently lifted Aaliyah's head taking the pillow from behind her.

The woman placed the pillow over Aaliyah's face and pushed down sucking all the air out. With her peaceful sleep now interrupted, her body went into fighting mode. It took a few seconds for Aaliyah to realize that it was the weight from a human body pressing down on her with a pillow that was causing her to not be able to breath. Her body began to jolt as she was mustering up the strength to fight the person off.

"Give it up and just die with some dignity," the woman uttered angrily. She pressed down harder, but the woman wasn't expecting Aaliyah to have so much fight left in her since she'd been heavily medicated. But the medication was wearing off and with Aaliyah's determination to live her adrenaline was on ten.

With her upper body being immobile, Aaliyah decided to make use of the flexibility of her lower body. On the first try, she was only able to raise her legs up slightly. As her chest began to compress, Aaliyah knew she was running out of time and had to act fast or else she would die. She rested her mind and body in an almost still motion. This made the woman believe that Aaliyah had succumbed to being suffocated.

The intruder relaxed her grip believing the hard work was done and that was when Aaliyah went into action. With all her strength, she lifted her legs kicking the woman in the back of her head. The woman lost her balance releasing the pillow and Aaliyah pushed it off her face. She began coughing profusely to catch her breath and at the same time, looking around for anything to use as a weapon although it was hard for her to see due to the darkness in the room.

Once the intruder got her bearings together she went at Aaliyah with vengeance ready to finish what she started. Aaliayah could see the shadowy figure lunging at her so she reached for the closest thing, which was a metal container on the stand next to her bed. She flung it as hard as she could, catching the side of the woman's head.

"Oh shit!" the woman screamed out in pain. She backed up holding her head in pain. With no fight left in her, Aaliyah used her last bit of strength to press down on the call button hoping a nurse would come to her rescue. The woman was about to come at Aaliyah again, but noticed she was holding down the button. Realizing someone could show up at any minute, instead of pressing her luck she rushed out the room not wanting to risk being caught.

"Is everything okay?" Amy came in the room and said turning on the light.

"No!" Aaliyah belted. "Someone tried to kill me. They just ran out! Go stop them before they get away!" she demanded before reaching for the cup of water on the stand.

"I'll go see if I can stop them," Amy said before running out. Amy stood outside the door for a moment giving the intruder time to at least get off the floor before alerting hospital security. It wasn't until she saw the doctor and another nurse heading towards Aaliyah's room did she put her acting skills on full display.

"Is everything okay, Amy? You seem flustered," the nurse asked.

"I was on my way to find security."

"Security... what happened... why do you need security?" The doctor wanted to know.

"The patient woke up and informed me someone just tried to kill her," Amy explained.

"What! Get security right now and call the police," the doctor ordered, brushing past Amy to enter Aaliyah's room. "Are you okay?" he asked with concern.

"Hell no, I'm not okay. Someone came into my room and tried to suffocate me. What type of hospital you people running if someone can sneak they ass in my room and try to kill me," Aaliyah yelled between coughs.

"Here let me get you some more water," the nurse suggested taking Aaliyah's cup to refill it.

"Miss, I'm so sorry this happened. Security should be here any moment and we've called the police," the doctor said nervously.

"Did you track down the ballsy motherfucker

that tried to kill me? I told that other nurse the person just left."

"Amy is on it. I promise you, we are doing everything we can to track down whoever is responsible. I understand you're upset and you have every right to be, but can I please examine you. I want to make sure you're alright," the doctor said calmly.

"Sure examine me. Get it over with so I can get the hell outta here."

"I want you to get better too, but you're in no condition to leave yet."

"So you say." Aaliyah shrugged. "Wait!" Her eyes darted around the room. "Where's my mother!" she blurted as the craziness she had endured began to unfold rapidly.

"Your mother... so the other woman that was brought in is your mother?" the doctor asked, relieved that one piece of the puzzle had been solved.

"Yes, that's my mother. How is she?"

"What's your name, Miss?"

"My name is Aaliyah Mills Carter. Now answer my question... where is my mother and is she alive?"

Chapter Eight

Girl On Fire

"You looking much better. I think it's time you get out this bed and we go to work," Arnez told Maya before placing a bag on the floor.

"What's in the bag?"

"Some new clothes. I can't have you out in these streets looking busted, can I. Now get up, take a shower and get dressed," Arnez ordered.

Maya looked down at the bag then back up at Arnez. "What's the rush?"

"We need to get to the bank before it closes."

"The bank... why are we going to the bank?"

"Because you're going to withdraw every dollar you have in your account. And don't bother giving me a bogus number. I know exactly how much money you have and I want every cent. Checking, savings, and safe deposit box. After we clean out those accounts we'll be cleaning out the accounts at your other bank."

"So you want to leave me broke?" Maya frowned.

"With that rich father of yours you'll never be broke. You had more money in your accounts than I even expected."

"We made a lot of money together, why do you need all of mine?"

"Let's just say I have a high overhead. Including a private island and an entire staff I have to pay for." Arnez smiled.

"An island… you ain't got no damn island. Just admit you greedy and want to leave me with nothing. That's fuckin' foul, Arnez," Maya spit.

"Listen, I have to get out of town. Shit done got way too hot. Supreme is coming for me and with all the money at his disposal, he will find me. But I plan to be long gone and I need your cash to make it happen. No hard feelings. I'm only looking out for myself the same way you were when you sent Emory to kill me."

"You told Supreme that I was involved. My father will never forgive me. I will be a piranha to him and everyone else. My money is the only thing I have left."

"You'll figure it out, Maya. You always do," Arnez smirked. "Now go take a shower and get dressed," he said tossing the bag at her.

Maya grabbed the bag and headed towards the bathroom scheming all the way there. *If this motherfucker think he gon' take my money and throw me to the wolves he's fuckin' crazy. I had shit planned out and Arnez is trying to ruin everything. I have to figure this shit out before his bitch ass leaves me with nothing,* Maya thought to herself, getting into the shower and letting the hot water stream down her body.

As Maya lathered her body with soap she began to devise a plan, one that she believed would put her back in the driver's seat. After taking a long shower, Maya stepped out with her body and hair dripping wet.

"What are you still doing in here!" Maya screamed as if upset that Arnez was seeing her naked body although she didn't bother trying to cover herself up.

"You were taking a long time in the shower. I wanted to make sure you weren't trying to get out of making our bank stops."

"I'm not trying to get out of anything. I just wanted to enjoy the comfort of a little luxury since I'll be on skid row by this time tomorrow," Maya remarked, pretending to look around for something to put on. "What did I do with my towel," Maya said sounding annoyed.

In his head, Arnez was ready to leave town and be done with Maya but his lower head had absolutely no common sense. He couldn't contain being aroused by the wet flesh of curves prancing around the room in his face. He imagined that naked body riding his dick and reminiscing about how her moist lips would deep throat him until he bust off in her mouth and the icing on the cake was that Maya always swallowed.

"We got a little time before the banks close. Why don't we sweat out them sheets... I mean we were never at odds in the bed. That's where we got along the best," Arnez said proudly.

With her back turned away from Arnez, Maya smiled widely. She put herself out as bait and like she was counting on, Arnez wanted to bite. *Your so predictable, I hate people like you,* the Drake line played in Maya's head as she listened to Arnez practically beg for the pussy.

"You can't seriously expect me to have sex with the man who's trying to ruin my life! You can forget it!" Maya objected convincingly.

"I told you this ain't personal, strictly business."

"If it's business then you need to pay me for my services," Maya shot back.

Arnez paused and Maya could tell he was debating her proposition. "A'ight I'll hit you off with a lil' something."

"How much?"

"That depends on how good of a performance

you put on." Arnez had this sleek ass expression on his face like he had the game all figured out.

"Then I better put on for you." Maya winked her eye and walked away.

"Where you going?!"

"Calm down, papi. I wanna make sure I earn me a nice chunk of change. Stay right there, I'll be right back."

Arnez was feeling a bit anxious like something might not be right, but his third leg would not listen to his inner voice that had good sense. "Hurry yo' ass up!" he shouted.

Maya licked her lips seductively further diminishing Arnez's capabilities of making rational decisions. His only objective was getting in Maya's hotbox. A few seconds later, Maya came sauntering out the bathroom in the high heel pumps that Arnez had gotten for her to wear to their trip to the bank. The heel had her legs looking extra thick and curvy and accentuated the slight gap between her legs.

"Damn baby, I'ma miss this pussy," Arnez babbled taking off his clothes before Maya had even made it to the bed. "Come sit on this dick wit' yo' sexy ass. Them heels is a nice touch." He nodded as if he had come up with the idea himself.

"Slow down. Don't you want me to rock the mic first," Maya teased.

"Fuckin' right. Don't nobody know how to blow me like you," Arnez said, getting comfortable on the edge of the bed. He was ready to fill her mouth with

The Final Chapter

every inch of his manhood.

"Lay back and relax, baby. I'm about to earn every dollar then some," Maya boasted licking Arnez's hardened dick like a delicious candy cane.

At first Maya took her time licking Arnez's dick and massaging his balls simultaneously. Her head game was so ridic that Maya was about to put his ass to sleep. While he was nodding off getting caught up in the rapture, Maya was slipping off one of her heels. Initially Arnez had a grip on Maya's hair, directing her head with each stroke, but he had become completely enthralled, so his hands were now spread to the side totally making himself vulnerable.

Right when Arnez was about to doze off from pure sexual bliss, Maya bit down so hard on his dick, he went from feeling like he was starring in his own porno flick to entering hell. Before Arnez had a chance to shake off the excruciating pain of Maya's teeth trying to rip off his dick, he felt the stabbing of her heel pressing down on the side of his skull. Maya kept swinging the heel in his head while never letting go of the grip she had on his meat until she smelled blood.

Once Maya no longer heard Arnez howling from pain, she spit out his bruised and bloody dick. She grabbed the lamp from the nightstand and bashed that over Arnez's head until it broke. Although he was a battered bloodied mess, Maya knew Arnez wasn't dead, but he was knocked out cold. Not sure what else she could get her hands on to put him out of his misery, Maya came up with an alternative plan as she rushed to get dress.

Maya stepped out into the hallway, but didn't know which way to go. She had been stuck in the bedroom ever since Arnez brought her there after being treated by the doctor. She did know they pulled into a garage when they first arrived and that's where Maya headed.

Damn it's a lot of shit in here," Maya huffed, looking around for what she needed. She was getting anxious because she was unsure how much time she had. She put a decent beating on Arnez, but he could come to at any moment. Maya kept searching. She was ready to give up and come up with an alternative plan but then buried in the corner, she noticed exactly what she needed. "Bingo!" She beamed.

Relief, excitement, and fear had Maya's heart racing. She ran back to the bedroom to grab Arnez's wallet and cell phone. She then rushed to the living room to get the gallon of gasoline she found in the garage. She opened it and began pouring the gasoline on the sofa, the floor and anything else until the container was empty. Maya glanced around the room one last time as if rejoicing in her work. But she had one more thing to do before celebrating.

"Hello… hello… is anyone there?"

"Daddy, it's me!" Maya sounded hysterical.

"Maya what's wrong… where are you?"

"Arnez is trying to kill me. Please come get me, Daddy! I need your help!"

"I'm on the way baby girl. Where are you?"

"Please hurry before Arnez kills me! Pleaaaaase!" she cried before giving her dad the address from some mail that was lying on the table. She could hear her father still talking, but hung up the phone to make her situation appear dire. After going to make sure Arnez was still knocked out, Maya lit the match and watched as the house went up in flames.

"Burn in hell, motherfucker." Maya smiled before slamming the front door.

Chapter Nine

I Believe You

"Miss, I need you to take a look at these pictures and tell me if you recognize them as the people responsible for shooting you and your mother," Detective Garcia told Aaliyah.

"No, that's not her. I told you who is responsible for doing this to my mother and me. Her name is Maya."

"Take a look again," he insisted, shoving the mug shots of Nekesa and Adama in her face.

"I don't know them chicks!" Aaliyah hissed, shoving the pictures out of her way. "You need to find

Maya. Not only did she shoot my mother and me, I know it was her that came into my hospital room and tried to kill me," Aaliyah said angrily.

"I understand you've been through a lot, but I need you to calm down. In order for me to close this case I have to gather all the necessary information, starting with who is responsible for putting you in this hospital."

"I already told you who is responsible, but you acting like you don't believe me and I don't understand why."

"Because Miss Mills, we have two women in custody right now who I'm positive are responsible for what happened to you and your mother."

"Then you're positively wrong!" she shouted.

"You were shot; in a coma. It can be difficult re-calling certain things. That's why I'm asking you to take your time and really look at these pictures. It might help you remember things more clearly," De-tective Garcia asserted.

"If you don't get them fuckin' pictures out my face I'ma shove them down your throat," Aaliyah snapped.

"Relax," the detective suggested, putting his hand up and moving back.

"Now I understand why so many innocent people are locked up, 'cause ya' be force feeding shit until a motherfucker agree wit' you. If I didn't know for a fact that it was Maya's evil ass that tried to kill me, you might convince me that them two females whom I've never seen in my life is guilty."

"I'm not trying to send two innocent people to jail. I'm checking into all leads and following the facts."

"If that's true then go track down Maya's ass. Now if you can excuse me I have some phone calls I need to make."

"There will be a police officer posted right outside your door so no one will be able to harm you. If you remember anything else, please give me a call," Detective Garcia said handing Aaliyah his card. She looked up at him and folded her arms tightly. "I'll leave it on the table for you," he said placing the card down then walking out.

"Detective Garcia, how's the patient?" Amy inquired the second he came out of Aaliyah's room.

"We're working on some new leads. Tell me are you the one caring for Miss Mills?"

"Yes, I am."

"I know her condition has improved, but is she experiencing any side effects?"

"What sort of side effects?"

"I don't know, her memory or how certain things might have transpired."

"Definitely. Miss Mills went through a traumatic experience. In most cases when patients go through that they will have some level of memory loss. It's very common," she assured him.

"That's what I figured. Thanks for the input."

"Of course. If you have any other questions don't

hesitate to ask. I'm here to help." Amy smiled.

"Thank you. I'll be in touch."

Amy wanted to help Detective Garcia believe anything but the truth. It was more about protecting herself than anyone else. She decided to check on her patient to see what Aaliyah knew and possibly what she told the detective.

"Can I get you anything, Miss Mills?" Amy was doing her best to play the concerned nurse.

"Hold on a minute," Aaliyah said putting the phone down.

"I'm sorry. I didn't realize you were on a call."

"Nah, I don't need anything. But I would like to know when I'll be able to see my mother."

"I'm not sure. Honestly your mother isn't doing well. I don't think it's a good idea for you to see her."

"I didn't ask you what you think. As a matter of fact, get my doctor in here. I need to speak to someone who can tell me what they know not what they think." Aaliyah then continued her phone conversation not saying another word to the nurse.

What a bitch! Too bad your ass didn't die. But you'll get yours if I have anything to do with it, Amy thought to herself, but instead said sweetly, "I'll go find your doctor."

"Yeah, you do that," Aaliyah said cynically. She waited for the nurse to leave then continued talking. "I have no confidence in these idiots. I don't trust that moron cop to track down a lost puppy let alone Maya," she complained to Supreme.

"Aaliyah, don't worry about Maya. I will find her. You focus on getting better."

"Daddy, I'll be fine. When are you coming?"

"I'm driving now. I have to stop and get your brother then we'll be there."

"Great! See you soon." When Aaliyah hung up with Supreme she called Nico. His phone went to voicemail so she then called her grandfather and his phone went to voicemail too. "Damn, ain't nobody answering they phone!" Aaliyah slammed down the phone before picking it right back up.

"Hello."

"Dale, is that you?" her voice was so low as if she couldn't believe someone finally answered her call.

"Aaliyah... Aaliyah is that you?"

"Yes, it's me."

"Oh my fuckin' goodness! You know how worried I've been. Where are you?"

"At the hospital in New York."

"The hospital? What are you doing at the hospital? Are you hurt... what happened?"

"Maya happened. She's the reason my mother and me almost died. I'm still waiting to speak to the doctor so I can find out what's going on with my mom."

"Baby, I'm so sorry you had to go through that. I'ma get on the next flight so I can be with you."

"You don't have to do that, Dale. I know you have mad business you handling. I just wanted to hear your voice and let you know that I was okay."

"Business can wait. There's no other place I want to be then by your side. I'll let you know when my flight lands. See you soon, baby."

Aaliyah was relieved that Dale didn't listen to her when she told him not to come. The last thing she wanted to do was come across as needy, but deep down inside she did need Dale. Aaliyah was seething over what Maya had done, but she was also feeling alone and scared... scared for her mother. Part of her wanted to break down and cry, but Aaliyah knew she had to be strong if not for herself then for her mother.

"Maya, what happened to you?!" Quentin questioned, immediately noticing the self-inflicted bruises on Maya's face.

"Oh, Daddy! I've never been so happy to see you." The tears were flowing rapidly as Maya was playing the role of victim to the hilt. She buried her face in his chest.

"Did Arnez do this to your face!" He held Maya's face up, distraught with how bad she looked, unaware that his daughter used her own fist to achieve a black eye and busted lip. "Where is that sonofbitch! I'ma kill him!" Quentin was becoming angrier by the minute.

"Let's just get out of here," Maya whined.

"Not until I get my hands on Arnez." Quentin would not budge.

"It's too late."

"What do you mean it's too late?" Quentin was puzzled. He didn't understand what Maya meant.

"Daddy, I had no choice... he was going to kill me! Please, Daddy forgive me... it wasn't my fault." Maya's tear game was top notch.

"Tell me what happened, Maya." Quentin held her shoulders tightly, staring her directly in the eyes.

Maya swallowed hard as if devastated about what she was ready to reveal. "I called you back and had you meet me here because..." Maya gave a dramatic pause.

"Because what... tell me now, Maya!" Quentin barked, a mixture of frustration and fretfulness in the tone of his voice.

"After I managed to free myself and was trying to get away, Arnez grabbed me and started punching me in the face. We struggled and as I was trying to get away, I knocked over a candle and the curtains caught on fire. Next thing I know that house is burning down."

"What happened to Arnez?"

"During our struggle, I hit Arnez over the head with a lamp to get him off of me. It knocked him out."

"Did he make it out the house?"

Maya shook her head no. She then put her head down and let more fake tears come down.

"It's okay, Maya. You did what you had to do. It was self defense."

"But nobody will believe that. With the trouble I've had in the past..." More tears.

"Don't cry, sweetheart. I believe you." Quentin pulled Maya in closely and rubbed her back lovingly. "It will all work out."

"No it won't, Daddy. Everybody hates me. Even though Arnez is a monster, people will still blame me because I'm an easy target."

"Don't you worry. I won't let anything happen to you. The police or no one else needs to know what happened. You're a victim and I'll do everything in my power to protect you."

"You promise, Daddy?" Maya gave her best angelic stare.

"I promise, sweetheart. You've been through enough and I won't let anyone else hurt you again."

Quentin held Maya even tighter, wanting to shield his daughter from any more unnecessary pain. She snuggled her head even deeper into his chest, with a deceitful smile engraved on her face the entire time.

Chapter Ten

There's Still Hope

Skylar watched from a distance as Talisa took a swim in the tranquil ocean water. Her body glided over the calm waves as if she belonged there like a mermaid. She stared in awe and in consternation. There was the woman that even in death still held the keys to Genesis's heart. Although Skylar always felt a twinge of jealousy about the woman who would forever be the unspoken third person in any relationship Genesis had, it was tolerable knowing that person was dead. But now all that had changed.

"You're not getting in?" hearing Talisa's voice

shook Skylar out of her faraway thoughts.

"Not right now. I think I'm going to sit here and enjoy this breeze and ocean view a little while longer."

"Isn't it beautiful. I always say this place is like having a little piece of heaven in hell," Talisa said with a slight smile. "But I would be more than willing to give it up if I could get back to my husband and child. Have you come up with any ideas on how to escape?"

"Not yet, but trust me, a second isn't going by where I'm not trying to figure out a plan. I refuse to live the rest of my life on an island no matter how picturesque it is."

Skylar wasn't exaggerating. She was literally spending every second plotting her escape. Even while sleeping, the contemplations dominated her dreams. For the last few weeks she had been observing the movements of everyone. When Skylar first arrived she noticed that there was a tightly run operation in place. One man by the name of Julio seemed to be in charge. The staff would follow his orders without hesitation. But in the past few days there appeared to be some discord and Skylar wanted to know why. If it continued, that could be her way out. All she needed was one weak link to help plot her escape with.

"Any luck with locating Angel?" Genesis asked Nico as they sat on the private rooftop balcony discussing business.

"Nothing concrete. I've received some possible leads that she's supposed to be marrying Blaze soon."

"What! Are you sure?"

"That's the word I'm getting. I hate that a daughter of mine is marrying that man. I'm sure Angel has no idea what sort of person he is. He has no honor." Nico put his head down, fighting his frustration.

"Do you think Blaze has any idea that Angel is your daughter?" Genesis questioned.

"I don't see how. Only a handful of people know. But then again, I can't put anything past that guy. I'll tell you one thing, if by chance he did get a hold of that information, he hasn't told my daughter."

"That would even be low for Blaze. We did a lot of business with that man and looked out for him. With everything that transpired, at some point he would have to put his anger aside and do the right thing. I mean we're talking about reuniting a father and daughter. He can't be that lowdown."

"Yes, he could," Nico disagreed. "A man who is dishonorable in business is capable of anything. But I will find Angel. Blaze or any one else is going to keep me from my daughter. I can promise you that. I plan on going back to Miami so I can stay on top of things. But I'm not leaving until I find out what's going on with Aaliyah and Precious. I refuse to believe they're dead."

"I don't want to believe it either," Genesis said solemnly. "But we do have to prepare ourselves. Maya and Arnez are both disturbed individuals. We can't put anything past them."

"I get that. But if Aaliyah and Precious were dead, I would feel it right here," Nico said putting his right hand over his heart. "I know shit ain't right, but not dead."

"I feel you on that," Genesis said thinking about Talisa. He wondered if he could feel her presence being alive or if he had resigned himself to believing that she was dead for so long that that connection no longer existed. "I know whatever the answers are, Nico, you won't stop until you get them."

"You damn right. As a matter of fact, let me call the investigator that I have working on it. See if he has any updates," Nico said reaching for his cell phone. "I have three missed calls from an unknown number. Damn, I didn't realize I had my phone on silent. I wonder who it could've been," Nico wanted to know.

"I'm sure if it's important they'll call back." Right after Genesis spoke those words, Nico's phone began ringing.

"You might just be right," Nico looked at Genesis and said before answering. "Hello."

"Daddy, is that you?"

"Aaliyah!" Nico's eyes instantly watered up.

"Yes, it's me Daddy."

"Aaliyah, baby how are you… where are you?"

A smile crossed Genesis's face when he realized Nico was speaking to Aaliyah. His friend had been through so much and for him to finally get some good news was truly a blessing.

"I'm at the hospital. Daddy, so much has happened. Are you here in New York?"

"Yes! I wasn't leaving until I found out what happened to you and your mother."

"Then please come to the hospital so I can tell you everything that's happened. I really don't want to talk about it over the phone."

"Say no more, baby girl. Tell me what hospital you're at and I'm on the way." After Aaliyah gave Nico the information he hung up and Genesis could see the stress evaporate from his face.

"Man, I'm so happy for you," Genesis said giving Nico a hug.

"Genesis, you know I don't do a whole lot of praying. But these last few weeks, I've never spent so much time on my knees begging God to bring my family back to me. I've finally got a sign that He's been listening."

"Of course God's listening. He's going to bring Angel back to you too. Just wait and see."

"You're right. I believe that in my heart too. Why don't you come to the hospital with me? I know Aaliyah would be happy to see you."

"I appreciate the offer, but you give Aaliyah my best. Tell her me and Amir will be stopping by soon, but you go spend some alone time with your

daughter. I know you need that." Genesis smiled warmly.

"You're right, I do. Thanks, man."

"Did Aaliyah say anything about Precious?"

"No, but I'm assuming she must be there with her. Aaliyah said she didn't want to get into all that over the phone," Nico explained.

"That's understandable. Well, keep me posted. I'ma call Amir and let him know what's going on. I know he'll be so relieved that Aaliyah is alive and well."

"Yeah, you do that and I'll call you when I get the details about everything," Nico said before rushing off to the hospital.

Genesis stood in silence after Nico left looking out at the New York City skyline. Witnessing Nico go from a state of mourning to exultation in a matter of minutes gave Genesis that sense of optimism he was trying to suppress. Neither one of them wanted to admit it, but it seemed extremely plausible that both Aaliyah and Precious were dead. If they were able to survive the wrath of Maya and Arnez, then Genesis hoped that maybe Talisa had the same fate.

Chapter Eleven

The Clock Is Tickin'

"Amir, we've been waiting for over two weeks to get our product. We can't go any longer without it," Markell, a long time buyer said to Amir.

Amir put down his glass of water before speaking. He decided to take another swallow to give him more time to debate what he would say next. He had to choose his words carefully as he didn't want to make an already disgruntled buyer even more irritated.

"We've always given you the best product at the best prices. Our latest shipment has been delayed but we got confirmation today that it's in route," Amir lied.

Markell's poker face was strong so Amir wasn't sure what was going on in his head. Markell's blank stare was making him uncomfortable probably because Amir knew he was lying and wondered if the man sitting across from him knew too.

"Can I get you gentleman anything else?" the waitress asked, catching Amir off guard.

"I'm good. What about you, Markell?"

"I'll have another one of these," Markell replied holding up his empty glass. In a way, the fact that Markell wanted another drink put Amir at ease.

"I'll be back shortly with that drink." The waitress smiled taking Markell's glass.

"Amir, you know I've done business with your father for a few years and I have a great deal of respect for him. I like you too. You're smart."

"Thank you."

"But my people are hurtin' right now. They need product. If they don't have none then they can't eat. We both know how niggas get when they hungry. Shit gets real chaotic, quick."

"I understand that."

"Are you sure?"

Amir nodded his head acknowledging he was well aware what Markell was saying.

"If you understand, then you also grasp how critical it is that what you're saying to me is true. So the shipment is in route as we speak?"

"It is."

"Then when will it be here?"

"Give me a week." Amir reached for his glass before realizing it was empty. He put it back down and rubbed his hands together trying to divert from the fact that he was lying. The truth was, Amir had no idea when they would receive the next shipment. All he could do was try to buy more time.

"A week.... I can give you that," Markell said taking his drink from the waitress. "But a week is all I got. After that, I'll have to go elsewhere for product. I don't wanna have to do that."

"And you won't have to. You will get what you need."

"I better because when product get low, that's when niggas start stepping on shit to make it stretch. Then customers begin to OD and of course that make police take a closer look at what's going on in the streets. I don't need that type of heat on me."

"I get what you're saying and that's why I'm going to get you what you need. I got..." Amir paused while he was speaking as if something had caught his attention.

"You got what?" Markell asked, baffled as to why Amir stopped speaking abruptly. "Amir!" Markell spoke loudly wanting to get Amir's attention back on their conversation.

"My fault, Markell. But can you give me one second," Amir said standing up. "I see someone that I really need to speak to." Before Markell could protest,

Amir was gone.

"This nigga here." Markell shook his head before ordering another drink.

Amir made a beeline to his target before she had a chance to leave. "Justina, wait!" he yelled out as she was walking out the door.

"Daddy, wait. Someone's calling me." Both T-Roc and Justina turned to see who it was.

"Justina, hey. I thought I was gonna miss you," Amir said slightly out of breath from rushing to try and catch up with her. "Hey, T-Roc." Amir reached out to shake his hand. "It's always good to see you."

"Same. How's your father? I need to stop by and see him."

"He's hanging in there. We got a lot going on right now."

"Yeah, I know, but it'll work out," T-Roc said with confidence. "Justina, I'll be in the car." He kissed her on the forehead. "Tell Genesis I'll be coming through soon," T-Roc said, turning his attention back to Amir.

"Will do." Amir nodded his head.

"I'll be out shortly." Justina told her father before he turned to leave

"Take your time. I have a few calls to make."

"Wow, Amir you're the last person I expected to run into."

"I was meeting someone for lunch," Amir said looking over at the table Markell was sitting at. "Had some business to discuss."

"I see. So how have you been?"

"You'd know if you would answer my calls. Why have you been ignoring me, Justina?"

Justina glanced down at the marble floors in the upscale Upper East Side restaurant before glancing back up at Amir. "Sorry about that, but I've been dealing with a lot lately."

"So have I. I'm sure you've heard about Aaliyah and her mother."

"I have. My dad mentioned it to me. I'm really sorry, Amir. I know how close the two of you are."

"Yeah, well I remember how close all three of us used to be."

"True. Those were the good old days, but now it seems like a lifetime ago. I guess it's too late now for us to get those days back," Justina said somberly.

"I don't believe that. I haven't given up."

"But Aaliyah's dead."

"Don't say that!" Amir barked before catching himself. "I apologize. I didn't mean to come at you like that."

"It's okay. I know more than anyone how much you care about her."

"I care about you too, Justina."

"I know you do. I honestly hope you're right about Aaliyah not being dead. I was too hurt to admit it before, but it would be nice if we could get our clique back together." Justina gave a bashful smile.

"So would I."

"It was good seeing you, but I really should be going. I'm sure my dad is done making his phone calls by now." Justina laughed.

"I'm sure he is too. I'm glad we had a chance to talk though, but don't be a stranger. If you see me calling it's okay to answer."

"I will." She giggled nervously. "I'll talk to you later and if you get some good news about Aaliyah let me know."

"I will, but I can't let you go without giving me a hug." Justina reached over and hugged Amir. "By the way, you look beautiful," he said letting her go.

"Thank you." She blushed.

Amir stared out the floor to ceiling glass window watching Justina get in the tinted SUV. She looked even more stunning than when he saw her a few months ago. The tie-dye dress with a plunging neckline, crisscross back, and front slit accentuated curves that no one besides Justina knew she even had. Her hair was up in a French roll with loose curls framing her face. Amir was intrigued with how she had made this transition from being a naturally pretty girl next door to glam doll. He couldn't help but wonder what or who was the motivation behind Justina's burgeoning beauty.

With Amir being completely enthralled dissecting Justina he almost didn't hear his phone ringing. "What's up, Dad?" he answered.

"I got news about Aaliyah." Amir was tempted to end the call right then unwilling to hear anymore bad news about the woman he one time thought would be his wife.

"Dad, whatever it is, I don't want to hear it."

"She's alive, Amir."

"What did you just say?"

"I said, Aaliyah is alive. I was here when Nico got the call. She's in the hospital, but she's fine. Amir, are you there?"

"Yeah, I'm here," Amir finally said after being left speechless with the news. "What hospital is she at?"

Once Genesis gave his son that information, Amir ended the call and headed straight to the hospital to see Aaliyah.

Chapter Twelve

Either You With Me Or Against Me

"The thought of never hugging you again had to be the scariest feeling in the world for me," Supreme said holding Aaliyah tightly.

"He's not exaggerating, Aaliyah. I've never seen Dad that shook up before. We're so happy to have you back," Xavier said, smiling at his sister. "Now if only mom would wake up."

"She will," Aaliyah said, trying to sound optimistic.

"She better. We were finally becoming close and now she's been ripped away from me. I want my mother in my life." The resentment in Xavier's tone was evident.

"Son, this is the time we have to let go of the negativity and be positive. Your sister is alive and your mother will survive too. We all know what a fighter she is. That ain't changed. Precious needs to know we fighting for her too."

"Dad is right, Xavier. Mom is like a cat with nine lives. She'll get through this."

"Aaliyah, if you don't mind, I'ma go sit with your mom for a minute."

"Of course not, Dad. I think you should be with her. If anybody can bring Mom out of a coma, it's you." Aaliyah smiled.

"I don't know how he does it," Xavier commented once Supreme had left Aaliyah's hospital room.

"How he does what?"

"Keep going on this bullshit cycle over and over again. They're not even married anymore and she's still breaking his heart. Why did she have to go after Maya by herself? She should've waited for help. She's just as stubborn as everyone says!" Xavier yelled in frustration.

"She was trying to save my life."

"And look where it got her. In a hospital bed about to die. Was she thinking about me?"

"Where is this coming from?" Aaliyah was confused.

"You've always had a close relationship with Mom. She's always been there for you. They got a divorce when I was young. I was basically raised by Dad. I love him and I couldn't have asked for a better father, but I needed my mom too and she wasn't there."

"Xavier, I know it was hard growing up without her being there all the time, but mom has always loved you. She just thought that Dad would be better at raising a man and she was right. Look how you've turned out. You've been accepted by every Ivy League university. Not only are you super smart, but you're also an incredible athlete. Everything Mom wanted for you came true."

"That sounds cool, but I'll give it all back if I can have my mother. I want her to live to see me be great. When she came to LA to see Dad and me I finally believed that the relationship I always wanted with my mother would happen. Then I came to stay with her here in New York and it was perfect. I just don't understand why she couldn't have waited and let me, Dad, or even grandfather come with her. We could've helped take Maya down," Xavier seethed.

"Mom is who she is and everything she does is out of love for us. She saved my life, Xavier. If she hadn't of showed up when she did, I would dead."

"You're right and I'm sorry."

"Don't be sorry. I know you're lashing out because you're scared. I'm scared too. If she doesn't make it..." Aaliyah's voice cracked and her eyes teared up. "I'll blame myself. Unfortunately, I have some of those same stubborn traits as our mother. If I hadn't of broken into Maya's apartment, her and Arnez wouldn't have had an opportunity to hold me hostage."

"Stop it! I'm not gonna let you do this. The only person to blame for all this bullshit is Maya... point blank. And she will pay for what she's done even if I have to kill her myself!" Xavier exclaimed.

Aaliyah had never seen that side of her brother before and it made her uncomfortable. There were enough killers in the family and she was hoping that gene had bypassed her little brother. Before she could speak on her concerns, Nico and Quentin walked in her room together.

"Dad, grandfather! I'm so happy to see you both!" Aaliyah beamed, hugging both men.

"I'ma have as many gray hairs as Quentin dealing with you and your mother," Nico said squeezing Aaliyah tightly.

"I'm sorry I didn't get here sooner, but by the time I heard your message I was in the middle of handling something important. But I got here as soon as I could," Quentin explained, embracing his granddaughter.

"No worries, grandfather. I'm just happy you're here."

"There's no other place I'd rather be. And unlike Nico, I'm already fully gray, so I suppose the only thing stress can do to me at this point is send me to an early grave." Quentin laughed.

"Well we can't let that happen, grandfather. We wouldn't know what to do without you." Aaliyah held her grandfather's hand tightly, elated to see him again.

"We spoke to the doctor before we came in, but he couldn't give us any updates on Precious. I'm about to go see her, but I wanted to stop in here first," Nico explained. Before Aaliyah could tell her dad that Supreme was already in the room with Precious, he was walking out and Detective Garcia was coming in.

"Miss Carter, I have a few more questions about the intruder you had."

"What intruder?" Quentin questioned becoming alarmed. Aaliyah had already told Xavier what had happened so he wasn't taken aback by what the detective said like their grandfather was.

"Maya came to my room earlier today and tried to kill me yet again." Aaliyah frowned, folding her arms. "I guess she wanted to give it another try since she came up short the first time. But she gon' learn to stop fucking wit' me." Aaliyah pointed her finger as if chastising a child, with no regard to the detective standing a few feet away.

"This happened earlier today?" Quentin wanted to confirm.

"Yes, today. Somehow her trifling ass must've found out we were at this hospital, so she decided to attack. I attacked that ass right back," Aaliyah smacked, turning her attention back to Detective Garcia. "What other questions do you have for me, detective? I done gave you everything but Maya's damn social security number. What more do you need?"

But instead of answering Aaliyah's question, the detective turned towards Quentin who he could see had something heavy on his mind. "Sir, is there anything you need to tell me?" the detective asked.

Quentin glanced over at his granddaughter then back at the detective. "No, I don't have anything to say."

"Are you sure?" the detective persisted.

"Grandfather, if you have something to say you should say it. Like do you know where Maya is? Her ass need to be locked up ASAP before she try to sneak in my room again."

"I got you covered. You don't have to worry about that, sis," Xavier spoke up and said with a quickness.

"Miss Carter, I have a police officer posted right outside your door. No one will be able to harm you. I promise. But, sir, your granddaughter is right. If you have something to add that will help with my investigation, please share," Detective Garcia said.

"Yes, grandfather do share."

Quentin hesitated for a moment before opening up. "The truth is there is no way Maya could've come here today."

"What the fu..." Aaliyah stopped herself before she cursed at her grandfather. "I can't believe you are still defending Maya! Do you not see me in this hospital bed and your other daughter is in a coma."

"Aaliyah, I would never cover for Maya when it comes to you. You know how much I adore you."

"Then why are you lying to the detective saying Maya didn't come into my room today?"

"Because it simply isn't possible."

"Sir, please explain yourself," Detective Garcia pressed.

"Because Maya was with me."

"That's bullshit!" Aaliyah spewed, no longer giving a fuck that she was cursing at her grandfather. "Maya was here today trying to kill me! How dare you lie for her!" Aaliyah screamed.

"Aaliyah, calm down." Xavier walked over to his sister's bedside and placed his hand on her shoulder. "Don't get upset."

"How can I not be upset?! Grandfather is not only defending that loco daughter of his, but now he's lying for her too."

"Grandfather, Aaliyah is right. It's one thing to defend Maya, but it's another to lie for her especially when you know she's the reason why my sister and mother are in this hospital right now."

"I would never in my life lie for Maya when it came to either one of you. What I'm saying is true. Maya called me earlier today and asked me to pick her up. She was in upstate New York. She was bruised and battered at the hands of Arnez. I went and got Maya and she has been with me until I came to see you at the hospital. So there is no way possible she was able to come here and try to kill you, Aaliyah."

The room went quiet as everyone absorbed
what Quentin said. Based on his story, it was humanly
impossible for Maya to be in two places at the same
time. There was no reasonable explanation, but
Aaliyah wasn't trying to hear it.

"Maybe you have the day or the time wrong, I
don't know. But it was Maya... I know it was her!"
Aaliyah was adamant.

"Sir, I'm going to need you to come down to the
station so I can take your statement. I'm also going to
need to speak to your daughter, Maya."

"That's fine. We'll meet you at the police station
with my attorney," Quentin let it be known. "Now
if you would excuse us, I would like to speak to my
grandchildren privately."

"I can do that, but I'll be waiting right outside,"
the detective said and left.

"I cannot believe you, grandfather!" Aaliyah
shook her head in disgust. "I'll never forgive you for
this. You have some nerves lying for that monster
you brought into this world."

"Aaliyah, stop! I want Maya brought to justice
too, but one thing I do know is how much grandfather loves you. He would never lie to protect Maya if
it meant hurting you."

"Thank you, Xavier."

"Don't thank me, grandfather. Personally, I wish
you wouldn't have told that detective anything that
would take his eyes off of Maya. She's a problem that
needs to be dealt with."

"I'm well aware how everyone in this family feels about Maya. But the truth is the truth."

"If that's what you believe then start walking in your truth. Your daughter is fucked up! My mother might die because of Maya! I'm in this hospital because of Maya. Or don't you believe that either?" Aaliyah screamed.

She was waiting for her grandfather's response because all she got was silence. Quentin took a little bit too long to answer the question for Aaliyah's taste so she was done. "I need you to leave."

By the expressions on their faces, neither Xavier nor Quentin were expecting to hear those words come out of Aaliyah's mouth, but she meant it. "You heard what I said, I need you to leave."

"Aaliyah, don't do this. I love you more than anything, Don't do this, please," Quentin pleaded.

"You obviously don't love me enough to believe what I'm telling you about Maya. And I don't want you coming anywhere near me until you do."

"Aaliyah, you don—"

"Get out!" Aaliyah belted, cutting her grandfather off before he could finish his sentence.

"Grandfather, I think it's best you go." Xavier could see that things were going from bad to ugly very quickly so he wanted to shut things down before it got even worse.

"I'll leave, but Aaliyah please know that I'll never turn my back on you. I'm here whenever you need me."

Aaliyah looked away refusing to acknowledge her grandfather. She had absolutely nothing left to say to him. Quentin walked out as if defeated.

"You know I always have your back, but I think you were a little too hard on grandfather," Xavier stated.

"At this point, I don't care. The line has been drawn. In this war against Maya, either you're with me or against me. Anybody fuckin' wit' Maya is against me, which means grandfather is the enemy.

Chapter Thirteen

The Time Is Now

Supreme stared lovingly at Precious not saying a word. He simply wanted to be near her. He stroked her hair and gently kissed her lips. To him she looked like a delicate flower lying in the hospital bed. It was easier for Supreme to see Precious that way than for him to admit that she appeared fragile and weak.

Supreme had watched the love of his life fight and win so many battles in her life, but for the first time he was afraid that Precious might not make it. He held her hand and closed his eyes.

"You've always had the softest hands," Supreme said caressing her long slender fingers. "I still remember the day I put the ring on your finger and we exchanged vows. No matter what we've been through, in my heart you've always remained my wife. I wish I'd told you that when you came to LA to see me. I'm sorry I pushed you away."

"Don't be sorry now."

Supreme turned around to see the face of the callous voice speaking to him. "I should've known it was you." He shrugged. "I'm trying to have a private conversation with Precious. Can you give me a few more minutes?"

"It takes two people to have a conversation," Nico remarked. "So no, I can't give you a few minutes, 'cause clearly you talkin' to yourself."

"You know what I meant. Besides, I'm positive Precious can hear and understand everything I'm saying." Supreme glanced over at Precious and squeezed her hand.

"I don't care what you meant. You always a day late and a dollar short. You so quick to declare your undying love for Precious when something tragic happens. But you the first one to cut her off when she disappoints you or isn't the perfect wife. You love putting Precious on a pedestal only to knock her off."

"I get it, Nico. You mad 'cause no matter how many times you put Precious first, you'll always be her second choice. That has to suck."

"Fuck you, Supreme!"

"Nigga, fuck you too," Supreme's casual tone only enraged Nico more.

"I want you out of her room," Nico demanded. Supreme chuckled at Nico's request.

"What is going on in here?" a nurse came in and asked.

"I want that man escorted out of this hospital room," Nico ordered. The nurse kept looking back and forth at both men not sure what to think.

"Miss, I was here first, trying to spend some quiet time with my ex-wife. This man interrupted me so if anyone should be leaving, it should be him," Supreme stated.

"Sir, is that true?" the nurse asked Nico.

"The truth is, Precious is my wife. We're married. So I get to decide who is allowed in this room and I want this man out."

"Sir, if this man is her husband, he does have the right to ask you to leave," the nurse informed Supreme.

"My daughter's in this hospital..."

"You mean my daughter," Nico corrected him.

"Our daughter is in this hospital and her mother is fighting for her life. The last thing I want to do is start drama in this room where Precious is trying to stay alive. So I'll let you have this, Nico. I'll leave but just know, I will be back."

"Yeah, you bet not let me catch you in here," Nico continued to yell while Supreme was exiting with the nurse. "That motherfucker makes my skin crawl," Nico mumbled taking a seat next to Precious. "If you able to hear any of this shit going on, I know you cursing me out," Nico said to Precious. "I know I shouldn't be showing out in this hospital, but you already know that nigga Supreme just bring out the worst in me." Nico kept shaking his head.

"If I had to be honest with myself, maybe Supreme ain't the one that I'm angry at, maybe I'm mad at you. For some fuckin' reason, you do always choose him. He is always your first choice. Even this time when you did choose me, when you got your memory back, you ran right back to Supreme. You get on my nerves wit' that shit, but yet I still keep loving you." Nico laughed. "I guess I have to laugh to keep from crying. But I tell you what. I rather you be alive and with Supreme than lying here or dead. I need you in my life, we all do. This world would not be the same without you in it. So please wake up, Precious, we need you," Nico said, resting his head on her stomach.

"Supreme, is that you?" Nico thought he heard Precious speak, but the sound was so low that he thought maybe his mind was playing tricks on him, until she spoke again. "Supreme... Supreme is that you?" Nico then felt Precious rub the top of his head with her hand.

"Precious, it's me, Nico," he said lifting his head up.

Her eyes were halfway closed and Precious

seemed to be struggling to open them. But that didn't keep her from mumbling Supreme's name over and over again. That shit hurt Nico to the core, but he put his pain aside and focused on the fact that Precious had come out of her coma.

Skylar stood outside the door where she could hear two of the guards having an argument with Julio. While being discreet so her presence went unnoticed, she listened intently to their heated conversation.

"We haven't been paid in weeks. I'm not working another day until I get paid," one of the guards threatened.

"Calm down, Gabe! You'll get paid."

"When, Julio? You keep telling us that, but I see no money."

"All your needs are being met. You eat good here. The two of you are living in luxury," Julio said.

"My family in back home can't pay their bills with food. I need cash," Gabe said rubbing his fingers together.

"He's right, Julio," the other guard agreed. "I need to send money home to my wife. She's pregnant. I haven't even been able to send for her because I have no money. I came here because you promised I would make lots of money."

"And you have made lots of money," Julio countered.

"Yes, but that money has been spent. I need new money because I have new bills. Bills don't stop they keep coming."

"Mario, I understand your frustration and—"

"I don't want your understanding," Mario cut in and stated. "I want my money. The money I was promised."

"Yeah, we both do," Gabe added.

"I'll get your money. Now please go check on the kitchen staff as dinner time is approaching," Julio demanded.

The two guards exchanged stares as if debating whether to follow Julio's order. Julio could see what was going on and tried to rein the men in before he lost control.

"Listen, the two of you still work for me. If you want to get paid, I suggest you do as I say."

"Okay, Julio, but you better have our money," Gabe said while Mario nodded his head. Skylar watched as they went out the back door and Julio quickly got on his phone.

"Arnez, where are you!" Julio barked on the phone. "I've been calling and leaving messages, but I get nothing. The staff hasn't been paid and they're threatening to leave. You need to call me ASAP! 'Cause if I don't get these boys some money soon, ain't nobody gonna be here to watch after your prized possession."

The Final Chapter

Julio ended the call and then began cursing in a Spanish language that Skylar didn't understand. But that was irrelevant, she understood enough to know there was a major division within the crew. Skylar knew she had to act fast. For whatever reason, Arnez was MIA and for all she knew he could be in jail or even dead. If the staff didn't get paid soon which seemed unlikely, Skylar knew the guards would bail. She and Talisa could possibly be stuck on the island forever.

Chapter Fourteen

We Need Answers

Maya had her blunt bob haircut slicked back in a low bun. She had on minimal makeup, not even wearing foundation to try and cover up her self-inflicted black eye. Her three thousand dollar navy blue Gucci pantsuit looked liked an off the rack no name item the way she had it paired with a plain white shirt and leather black loafers. But none of this was by accident. Maya wanted to ditch her normal straight off the runway glam exterior for a more demure, librarian girl appeal. The only reason anyone in the room would know that money wasn't an issue for her was by the thousand dollars an hour attorney flanked by her side.

"My client has answered all your questions. Clearly she is the victim and should be treated as such," Attorney Kaplan said with a straight face.

"Based on the statement that her father gave, your client does have a solid alibi for the day an intruder..."

"Alleged intruder," the attorney injected, "There is no evidence besides the word of young woman that is herself a victim and you yourself admitted, Detective Garcia, you had concerns about her state of mind due to her recent injuries."

Detective Garcia turned to the other detectives then back at the attorney. He wasn't expecting his own words to be used against him while interviewing Maya, but they were.

"The point is the victim, Miss Carter, stated that your client tried to kill her and her mother. Leaving both women for dead."

"Miss Carter also stated that Maya came into her hospital room and tried to kill her which has been proven to be a lie. If Miss Carter would lie about that incident, then it is highly likely she would lie about that accident. Furthermore, it is no secret that Miss Carter and my client have a very acrimonious relationship, which would give her motive to lie on Maya."

Detective Garcia let out a long sigh before leaning back in his chair. He then leaned forward flipping his pen on the table. He glanced over at the prim looking Maya who didn't look capable of committing the heinous crimes she was being accused of.

"For now this department will hold off on pressing charges against your client. Although Mrs. Carter has now woken from her coma, unfortunately her recollection of what happened that night is shaky. With Aaliyah Carter being the only witness at this time we'll continue to gather more evidence before deciding how to proceed."

"That's fine, Detective Garcia, but it should also be noted that my client shares the same acrimonious relationship with mother as she does with daughter. So before you decide to bring your weak case in front of a judge, I suggest you have more evidence then the word of Precious and Aaliyah Carter. If not, then this case will be thrown out before it even makes it in front of a jury," Attorney Kaplan said confidently. "Good day... let's go, Maya."

"Detective Garcia, I know you've heard terrible things about me and I'll admit, I've made mistakes in the past, but I didn't do this. It was Arnez Douglass. He's the one responsible for everything."

"That's enough, Maya. You don't have to defend yourself. As I stated, you're the victim. Now let's go." Attorney Kaplan took Maya's hand and led her out.

"What do you think?" Officer Klein asked once Maya and her attorney had left the interrogation room.

"Honestly, I'm not sure," Detective Garcia admitted. "I do know we need to drop the charges against those teenagers Nekesa and Adama. I guess they were telling the truth when they said it was a joyride gone wrong," the detective shrugged. "Other than that, I don't have the answers."

"You don't have the answers? I thought you had the answers to everything, at least that's what you always telling everyone in this department," Officer Klein joked.

"Funny, Klein, but I'm not sure. All parties involved are questionable. I'm beginning to wonder if there are any real victims in this bunch." Detective Garcia shook his head and tossed his pen down.

"I don't know how many more visitors I can take," Precious said, smelling the flowers Genesis brought her. "You all are showering me with so much love. Maybe I need to almost die more often." She laughed.

"No, I think we getting too old for this. The next scare might send all of us into an early retirement. And I ain't ready for that." Genesis smiled.

"Yeah, I don't want that to happen either. You know they say as soon as a man goes into retirement, he lets himself go. We don't need a tall, handsome, always dressed to perfection man like yourself going downhill fast. Now do we," Precious said giggling.

"I see getting shot again for what the third, fourth time hasn't taken away from your colorful sense of humor."

"I like that... colorful sense of humor. No, it hasn't, but I will say I'm starting to think the joke is on me. How is it that I can pretty much remember everything, except for the night that Maya tried to kill me and my daughter? How is that possible?"

"Precious, when you took that bullet for Supreme you lost your memory for months. You were just starting to fully get back to your old self when this happened. It's not surprising that you would experience another memory lapse after being shot again."

"My doctor already explained to me that a setback like this wasn't uncommon, but I don't care about medical statistics. I had an opportunity to put Maya's ass in jail for a very long time and fucked it up."

"You didn't fuck up anything."

"Yes, I did. I tried to pretend that I remembered exactly what happened in order to corroborate Aaliyah's story and just made shit worse. Now that detective on the case thinks I'm a complete liar and don't believe anything that comes out of my mouth. If Maya gets away with this again, I swear, Genesis, the minute I get released from this hospital, I'm going to track her down and kill her."

"Precious—"

"Save it!" Precious said cutting Genesis off. "I don't need you to be the voice of reason for me right now and give me all the reasons why I shouldn't kill Maya."

"I wasn't gonna say that. I agree with you, Maya has to go, but I need you to hold up. Not only because you need to get better before you go on a murder spree, but I need to track Arnez down and Maya might be the key to that."

"So you're still on this Arnez thing?" Precious sounded unmoved.

"It's not a thing. He called me."

"You spoke to Arnez... when?" That stirred her interest. Precious's posture in her hospital bed became straight and stiff, eagerly waiting to hear what Genesis would say next.

"He called not long after Skylar was taken in broad daylight."

"That's the day I wish I could forget." Precious put her head down, reflecting back to when those men came and snatched Skylar up, right in front of her face. "I still wish I could've done more."

"Arnez had Skylar's kidnapping well orchestrated. There was nothing you could've done."

"So you're sure it was Arnez behind the kidnapping?"

"I'm more than sure. Arnez confirmed it when he called. But there's more."

Precious raised her eyebrow and leaned forward. "More like what?"

"Arnez said that my wife Talisa is still alive and that he has her."

"What!"

"No one wants to believe me. They think Arnez is simply playing one of his sick mind games with me."

"I believe you!" Precious blurted out. "I remember when Maya made Supreme believe that I had left him. She set the shit up so lovely that it was pretty convincing. But in all actuality I was being held captive in a basement, with the help of Maya's brother. So trust me, given what I know about Maya and what I've heard about Arnez, that isn't farfetched."

"Thank you for believing me, Precious. When you keep hearing that what you're saying sounds crazy, you start believing it," Genesis divulged.

"I feel you on that. But I got yo' back, Genesis. What you need me to do?" Precious perked up, getting excited about helping Genesis bring down Arnez and Maya.

"Slow down, firecracker. The first thing I need you to do is focus on your health and strength. I don't want you having anymore setbacks."

"Okay, Genesis, I get all that. Let's fast forward to me being well and back at home. Then what do you need me to do?"

"Hold off on killing Maya. I'm not even sure if she knows where Talisa is, but I'm positive she knows how to track down Arnez. I'm a little concerned because I haven't heard anything from him since that phone call. Now that he's made it his business to let

me know that he's indeed alive, it's not like Arnez to stay silent. He would want to taunt me as much as possible. I can't help but wonder if something has happened to him."

"You think Arnez is dead?"

"I never thought I would say this, but I hope not. He might be the key to me getting my wife back. If he is dead, then Maya might be the only link since she's been working so closely with Arnez."

"Once again Maya has bought herself more time." Precious sighed. "But if she can reunite you with your wife, then it's worth it."

"I know how hard it has to be to let Maya live a little bit longer, so thank you for doing this. I'll never forget what you're giving up for me."

"I'm not giving up much. I'm simply giving you some more time. Don't think for one minute that I'm done with Maya. Thanks to you, she gets to live a little longer, but death will be knocking at her door very soon."

Precious slumped back in her bed and a smile spread across her face. She began envisioning the day she would finally be able to get rid of her diabolical sister once and for all.

Chapter Fifteen

Childhood Memories

"Amir, why do you keep looking at the door?" Aaliyah asked before taking another bite of her salmon. "You've barely even touched your food. Do you want the waitress to bring you something else?"

"No, my food is straight."

"Then why aren't you eating it?" she continued to question, while reaching over with her fork to get one of his marinated shrimp. "This is good," Aaliyah said of the flavorful shrimp scampi made of olive oil, vermouth, garlic, lemon and other herbs. "Maybe you should just pass me your plate. No sense in letting a good meal go to waste."

"I forgot about that limitless appetite of yours."

"Funny... there you go looking at the door again." This time Aaliyah turned all the way around in her chair so she could see what had Amir's undivided attention. She almost spit out her food when she caught a glimpse.

"Sit back down," Amir said when Aaliyah practically jumped out her chair.

"You invited me to dinner knowing that snake was coming!" Aaliyah snapped. "I've only been outta the hospital for two weeks and this is what I have to be bothered with? Get the fuck outta here!"

"Please, Aaliyah. Give her a chance," Amir pleaded nervously seeing Justina approaching. "Thanks so much for coming." Amir quickly said, reaching over to give her a hug.

"I wasn't sure if I should come," Justina said looking over at an incensed-faced Aaliyah. "I see that I was right to be reluctant since obviously Aaliyah isn't happy to see me."

"Why would I be happy to see the person who was responsible for me spending almost a year of my life in jail? Not to mention you were aiming to have me rot in there for the rest of my life," Aaliyah mocked.

"Aaliyah, just hear her out. Can we all sit down please?"

"Fine, but make it quick!" Aaliyah flung her napkin down then sat back down.

"Aaliyah, I'm so sorry," Justina said sitting down in the chair across from her. "When I heard what happened to you it brought back all these memories from our childhood that I had suppressed. I missed my best friend. Then when Amir told me you were alive, I felt like maybe I would finally have a chance to make things right."

"Make things right? You tried to destroy my life, Justina."

"You're right. Jealously got the best of me. I was so hurt when I found out you and Amir were seeing each other. It felt like I had been betrayed by both of my best friends at the same time. Then when I got shot that night in Sway's hotel room, I really didn't know what happened at first. When I found out it was my own mother, it turned my world upside down. I chose her over doing the right thing and you had to suffer because of it. I'll never forgive myself for what I did to you, Aaliyah."

"We all made a lot of mistakes back then," Amir conceded.

Aaliyah cut her eyes at Amir. "Our mistakes didn't put anyone in jail.

"True, but our actions did bring unnecessary turmoil to someone we both claimed to love."

"It isn't the same, Amir!"

"You're right, Aaliyah. What I did is far worse than anything you and Amir did to me. I handled the situation so poorly and I would give anything to go back and do it differently. Unfortunately, I can't get a do over. All I can ask is for your forgiveness. I want a chance to make it right. For us to be friends again."

"You want us to be friends again?" Aaliyah rolled her eyes at the very idea.

"I know it would take time."

"You mean a lifetime," she huffed.

"Come on, Aaliyah. You know how hard it must be for Justina to come here and ask for your forgiveness when she knows that you'll probably shut her down."

"It's easy for you to defend Justina because she didn't try to ruin your life. I'll admit, I did feel guilty about my relationship with Amir. He was your boyfriend first, but that didn't stop me from going after what I wanted. The three of us have been friends ever since I can remember. We basically grew up together. For so long I considered you to be the sister I never had, but you messed all that up, Justina."

"I know." Justina put her head down in shame.

"That's the thing, you don't know!" Aaliyah shouted with fury. "That entire ordeal changed my life. It changed me as a person and not for the better. It made me resent the world and hardened me in the process. Maybe one day I can forgive you, Justina, but it won't be today."

"Aaliyah, wait!" Amir called out as Aaliyah grabbed her purse and hurried off.

"You should go after her," Justina suggested.

"No, it wouldn't help. When Aaliyah gets like this, it's best to leave her alone."

"It wasn't my intention to cause such an uproar by coming here. I knew there was a lot of bad blood between me and Aaliyah, but with so much time passing I thought that things would've got better."

"It was my idea for you to come. Things didn't go as smoothly as I would've liked, but I think you did right by coming. You at least cracked the door open by even getting Aaliyah to hear you out. She needs more time, but I think she'll eventually come around."

"You really think so, Amir?" Justina didn't sound convinced.

"Now, I didn't say how much time," he said laughing. "We both know it's easy for Aaliyah to get stuck in her ways, but she'll come around. I could tell when she was talking that the love is still there."

"I hope you're right because I want my bestie back."

"Dale! I'm so happy to see you," Aaliyah beamed when she entered her apartment and saw him sitting in the living room. "Why didn't you tell me you were coming?" Aaliyah asked, resting her head on his chest as they hugged.

"I didn't wanna tell you that I was coming like I did before. Then have to back out at the last

minute because something comes up. So I decided to surprise you."

"I'm definitely surprised in the best way possible. You feel so good, I don't want to let you go," Aaliyah said, holding on to Dale tightly.

"You feel good too, babe. I can't tell you how much I've missed you. I hated I couldn't come right after you called and told me you were in the hospital. Thank you for being so understanding."

"Baby, you found out your brother got killed. Of course I understood why you couldn't come. I'm still having a hard time believing Emory is dead. We had our differences, but I know how close the two of you were. Your brother had his ways, but there was no denying how much he loved you."

"Man, I keep waking up each day thinking this shit gon' get better, but the pain remains. He was all the family I had left. For him to be gone got me all fucked up." Dale sat down on the couch and buried his face in his fists.

"I would give anything to take your pain away. But baby in time, it will get better," Aaliyah said, stroking the side of Dale's chiseled face.

"It won't get no better until I find out who the fuck killed my brother. When I do, they a dead motherfucker."

"The police don't have any leads?"

"Nope. They so fuckin' clueless. If I wait around on the police, I might neva find out what happened to my brother."

"So what are you gonna do?"

"Get fuckin' street justice. Trust somebody know who killed Emory and for the right price they will talk. I just have to be a little patient."

"While you wait, let me make you feel better," Aaliyah whispered, kissing Dale's earlobe.

"You know what that does to me," he said, closing his eyes..

"That's the point." Aaliyah straddled Dale, sprinkling kisses from his earlobe to his lips then his neck and his chest as she unbuttoned his shirt.

"Damn, that feels good," Dale moaned, taking the nape of Aaliyah's hair and pulling it back as his tongue went wild until her hardened nipples were in his mouth. They were both so hot and bothered, they could've easily got undressed and had passionate sex in the middle of the living room floor, but Dale craved something more. He had been without his woman for so long that he wanted to love her down.

"Put it inside," Aaliyah purred in Dale's ear then arched her back as he cupped her breast before lifting her up. Dale carried Aaliyah into her bedroom, laying her down on the king-sized canopy bed. The French doors that opened up to the balcony were slightly open, causing the summer breeze to blow the white silk curtains. In the darkness of the night, the moonlight highlighted their naked bodies. The two lovers spoke no more words, instead becoming lost in their lovemaking.

Chapter Sixteen

It's My Way Or Die

Quentin was wrapping up his conversation with Maya's attorney when he heard a knock at the door. He wondered who could've gotten past security without him being notified, but when he looked out the peephole it made sense.

"You're the last person I expected to see," Quentin said when he opened the door. He reached out to hug his daughter, but was instantly shut down.

"I didn't come over here for a father/daughter reunion," Precious made clear. "Can I come in?"

"Of course. You know you're always welcomed here," he said closing the door.

"I wanted to let you know, I'm going to kill Maya. If you get in my way, I'll kill you too. I felt it was only right I let you know since you are biologically my father. Hopefully you'll stay out of it so I won't have to kill you, but we're all entitled to freedom of choice, so it's up to you."

"You wouldn't see me while you were in the hospital. Now you're out and instead of me having the opportunity to ask you how you're doing, you basically tell me that not only are you going to kill your sister, but you're willing to kill me too. Where did I go wrong as a father," Quentin said, pouring himself a drink.

"You see this bullet wound," Precious shot back, unbuttoning the first three buttons on her blouse revealing the bandage that was on her chest. "Maya did this to me. Don't fuckin' turn away! You look at it. This is what your daughter did. This is the last scar that Maya will ever leave on another human being. I'm going to put that deceitful bitch out of her misery once and for all."

"I can't listen to this," Quentin said abruptly, tossing back his whiskey before pouring another glass.

"You will listen! You've let Maya ruin your relationship with me and now your granddaughter. What more proof do you need that Maya is poison."

"Do you think I want this? Aaliyah won't even

take my calls. But what do you want me to do? I had no choice but to tell the truth. Maya was with me. She had nothing to do with what happened to Aaliyah in the hospital."

"I don't believe that but for argument's sake, let's say you're right. That doesn't negate the fact that Maya is responsible for Aaliyah's kidnapping and trying to kill her and me."

"You don't even remember what happened that night," Quentin reminded her.

"I don't need to remember. I believe my daughter. I know she didn't put this bullet in my chest."

"You know how Aaliyah feels about Maya."

"So what are you saying... you think Aaliyah is lying... that she's making this up?"

"All I'm saying is that if she's mistaken about what happened at the hospital then Aaliyah could be mistaken about who kidnapped her. Maya swears that Arnez is the person behind everything and that she was his victim too."

"Maya is a proven liar. They were partners. You know what," Precious said throwing up her arms. "I'm done trying to make you face the truth. I came and told you what I needed to say. So you go ahead and spend all the time you want with Maya while you can, before it's time for you to start preparing her funeral."

"I can't let you kill your sister, Precious."

"Maya is not my sister and like I stated when I got here. If you insist in getting involved with this, you'll end up dead too. So if you value your life, stay out my way."

Precious stormed out Quentin's building fuming. She really did love her father and although initially they had had a bumpy relationship, they had grown closer. All that changed because of Maya. She was losing her father and Aaliyah's once strong bond with her grandfather was crumbling and it infuriated Precious.

"Genesis, have you gotten any movement on Arnez?" she questioned while getting in her car.

"There might be some news. I'm waiting for a phone call now."

"Are you home?"

"Yeah, why?"

"I'm on the way," Precious said slamming the car door. Precious didn't even bother to wait for Genesis's response before pulling off. She was stuck on one thing... killing Maya and everything else was an afterthought. Precious wanted Genesis to locate Arnez ASAP so she could proceed with her plan to do what she should've done a long time ago. Murder Maya.

"Amir, what are you doing here," Aaliyah huffed letting him in.

"Was that Dale I saw leaving out?"

"Oh gosh, he didn't see you did he?"

"No. I was still in my car when he was coming out." Amir glanced around the apartment and noticed two glasses and plates with some leftover food. "Did he spend the night?"

"That's what a boyfriend typically does... spend the night with his girlfriend," Aaliyah mocked, tightening her bathrobe. "You still haven't told me what you want," she said walking over to the table to get her glass and finish the rest of her mimosa.

"I guess I'm surprised that dude is even fuckin' wit' you like that anymore."

"Excuse me! Why the hell would you say some dumb shit like that?"

"I don't know too many men that would still fuck with the girl whose father is responsible for killing their brother. I'm just saying." Amir shrugged.

"Come again?" The color seemed to drain from Aaliyah's face.

"Wait... you didn't know?" The stunned expression frozen on Aaliyah's face gave Amir his answer. "Wow, you didn't know."

"Are you saying my dad killed Emory?"

"That's exactly what I'm saying."

"You're a liar."

"When have I ever lied to you?"

"But why would my father kill Emory? That makes no sense. You... you.. you must be mistaken," Aaliyah stuttered.

"Supreme told all of us when he thought there was a very good chance that you and Precious were dead."

"But why?" Aaliyah continued to ask, shaking her head and covering her ears as if she didn't want to hear the reason why.

"Supreme found out that Emory was working with not only Arnez but also with Maya. I really did think you knew, Aaliyah. I figured Supreme had already told you," Amir said now wishing he had kept the information to himself.

"I knew Emory was shady, but I never thought he would stoop that low. Working with Arnez and Maya... that is scratching the absolute bottom of the barrel. Do you think Dale knew his brother was working with them?"

"I'm not a fan of Dale's, but I don't think he was in the loop. Emory was making those moves all on his own. But it don't even matter what side deals Emory was making, Dale will have a problem with whomever killed his brother."

"I have to figure this out. I have to make Dale understand why my father killed his brother," Aaliyah reasoned, going to the kitchen to make herself another mimosa.

"Aaliyah, you've always had a knack for making things work out in your favor, but you're setting yourself up for failure if you think you can explain this shit away to Dale. I suggest you end your relationship with that nigga now before the love he has for you turns to hate."

"I didn't ask for your suggestion," Aaliyah snapped. "You've always been jealous of my relationship with Dale so you would love if we broke up over this. But it's not gonna happen! Dale wouldn't hold me responsible for a decision my father made. He's not that type of man."

"Since you're so confident about that, I guess you'll be telling Dale that he can call off the search because you already know who killed his brother... your father."

Aaliyah bit down on her lip. It was taking all her strength not to throw the glass in her hand directly at Amir's head. Her hand was itching to do it. Unwilling to test her self control, Aaliyah placed the glass down on the table and walked away from it.

"Telling Dale won't help anything." Aaliyah fidgeted with her bathrobe as she imagined the contempt on Dale's face if she did tell him the truth.

"Is that your way of saying that I'm right?"

"You're taking way too much pleasure in my misery," Aaliyah scoffed. "Now that you've had your fun, you can go now."

"It wasn't my attention to get you rattled."

"Whatever, Amir," Aaliyah said cutting her eyes at him.

"I'm serious. I came over to apologize about last night. I wanted you and Justina to talk, but I probably could've handled things a lil' differently."

"Oh you mean like not bombarding me in the

middle of eating dinner."

"I'll admit, it wasn't one of my best decisions, but my intentions were good."

"I hear you, but nothing has changed since last night. I'm not ready to be friends with Justina again."

"But....."

"But seeing her again after all this time... was nice. Being around someone that I've known since I was a little girl, felt kinda good."

Amir's wide smile softened the tense mood in the room. "I won't push you, but at least I know you're open to the possibility of the two of you being friends again. That's what's up."

"Calm down, Amir. Justina is way, way down on my top ten list of priorities. Right now, Maya's name is occupying slots one through nine."

"Take what I can get. But let me go."

"Oh now you wanna rush off."

"I figured you'd be happy to see me go." He laughed. "On the real though, I have to go see my dad. We got some serious business to discuss."

"You not having no problems are you?"

"Between me and you, yeah we are," Amir confided.

"What happened?"

"Long story, but the cliff's notes version is, this new connect we've been using is mad late on our shipment. If we don't get some product soon, we gonna lose a lot of our long time customers."

"I had no idea it's gotten that bad."

"You were gone for awhile. Arnez did a number on us in more ways than one. I thought we were finally on an upswing, but we've been waiting on this shipment for weeks. Our buyers can't stall the streets much longer."

"What is your connect saying?" Aaliyah questioned.

"That's the crazy part, he done got ghost. The first couple weeks he was making excuses and promises. But the past week the motherfucker ain't saying shit. I don't know what the fuck is going on." Amir was scratching his head.

"With my situation being what it was, I haven't been caught up in that life for a minute, but it's nothing but a call. Dale is still using the same connect and they will deliver. Just say the word."

"I appreciate that, Aaliyah, I really do, but let's hope it don't come to that. We got a ton of money wrapped up in this deal. They've come through the last couple times, I'm hoping this is a small bump in the road."

"I'll keep my fingers crossed, but I'm here for you, Amir. Like I said, it's only a phone call."

"Thank you." Amir kissed Aaliyah on the forehead and left.

Aaliyah became lost in her thoughts the moment Amir was gone. She tried her best not to show it, but the news of her father killing Emory had her mind spinning. There was no doubt that Supreme had a valid reason for killing him, but Aaliyah knew it would never be good enough for Dale. She battled with her inner conscience wondering if she should come clean or let it be.

After they made love last night and this morning, Aaliyah felt closer to Dale than she had in a very long time. Even with the long period they had been kept apart, their bond remained intact. But she couldn't deny that deep down what Amir said resonated with her. No matter how much they loved each other, she wasn't confident their relationship could survive this. For now, Aaliyah decided to let it stay a well-kept secret.

Chapter Seventeen

Dangerous Game

"You can't be fuckin' serious!" Precious barked, tossing her purse on the couch. "Genesis, please tell me your source is wrong."

"I wish I could, but Arnez might really be dead this time. From what I'm hearing the stash house he had been staying at burned down in a suspicious fire and Arnez was inside, but didn't make it out alive."

"Are they sure?"

"No one has heard from Arnez since then. All of his business activities have come to a halt. It's gotten so bad that most of his workers have abandoned ship because no money is coming in."

"If Arnez is dead how much you wanna bet that Maya is behind it," Precious reasoned. "Didn't Quentin say that when he picked Maya up she had escaped Arnez? That she too had been his victim. That was the story she was spinning. It seems that it was actually vice versa. Maya is a piece of work."

"That may be true, but now Maya might be the only person that can tell me if Talisa is really alive and where Skylar is."

"Exactly! Why do you think I'm so pissed. There goes another reason why Maya gets thrown a lifeline. At this point, I think we should snatch her ass up and torture Maya until she tells us what we want to know," Precious decided.

"If only it was that simple. You and I both know that won't work with Maya."

"There's only one way to find out. Plus the added bonus is, it'll be fun watching her ass suffer."

"I'm leaning towards a different approach. No only that, Maya is well aware she's on our radar. If she hasn't gotten it for herself, I'm positive Quentin has security watching her twenty-four seven."

"Then what do you suggest we do, Genesis? Sit around and let Maya remain free to do whatever the fuck she wants."

"I'm not saying that. What I am saying is that Maya is on high alert. Every day she wakes up and every night before she goes to bed, she's expecting for all hell to break loose. Running up on her might be problematic."

"Problematic for who? Not for me."

"I understand your position, but you also need to understand mine," Genesis pointed out. "Quentin is no longer hands on, but he is a minority partner in our drug operation. Not only is he a business associate of mine, but he's also a friend. Snatching up his daughter and then possibly torturing her isn't ideal to me."

"Does the prospect of never knowing if your wife is still alive or locating Skylar more ideal to you?" Precious countered. "It's extremely doubtful that Maya will voluntarily give us the information we want. We have to get what we need by any means necessary."

Genesis paced across the hardwood floors in deep thought. Precious had a valid argument, but he wanted to believe there was another option however, he was stuck and couldn't think of any.

"We'll try it your way," Genesis agreed.

A smiled crept across her face as Precious began devising a scheme to enforce her plan.

Maya fought with her hair as her reflection glared back at her. She desperately wanted to wear it in its free natural curly state or pull out her flat iron and wear it bone straight. But Maya did neither. Not because she didn't want to, but because she chose to play it safe. She thought it would be the wrong move to jump back into her glam gal ways. She was still playing the role of the distressed, meek victim. It was much too soon to be whipping out her hair and accentuating her cheekbones with some Anastasia Beverly Hills So Hollywood highlighter. Instead, Maya put her hair back in a bun, but pulled out her Sepia lip gloss to bring a little life to her rather blasé appearance.

"For now this will have to do," Maya mouthed while internally she was counting down the days she could ditch the drab and go back to being fab. As she was putting on her final coat of lip gloss she heard the doorbell. "Oh fuck, that must be my dad," she moaned, taking her time to answer the door.

"I was beginning to think you weren't home," Quentin said when Maya opened the door.

"I'm sorry, Daddy. I had my music on while getting dressed so it took me a moment to hear the door. Please come in! I'm so happy to see you," Maya beamed, hugging her father.

"You're looking much better, how are you feeling?" Quentin asked as he walked hand in hand with his daughter.

"I'm doing my best to put the craziness behind me and get my life back. It's difficult, but each day that passes it seems a little easier, especially having

your love and support," Maya gushed squeezing her father's hand as they sat down on the couch.

"I'm happy to hear that. You know I only want the best for you, Maya."

"I know that, Daddy and I love and appreciate you for it." She smiled warmly. "Forgive me for my rudeness, can I get you something... water or juice?"

"No, I'm fine," he said patting her knee. "Of course I wanted to check on you, but I also wanted to speak to you about some concerns I have."

"Of course. What is it, Daddy... is something wrong?"

"I spoke to Precious the other day and she brought up some points that resonated with me."

"What kind of points?" Maya asked, as if she didn't have a clue.

"I know that you were with me the day someone came into Aaliyah's hospital room, but she's adamant that you were the one that held her hostage for all that time. I know how she feels about you, but I can't imagine my granddaughter lying to me or her mother about something so critical. I'm giving you an opportunity to tell me the truth, Maya, before things get completely out of hand. I'm your father. Whatever you tell me won't make me love you any less."

Maya stared deeply into her father's eyes and then stood up, turning away dramatically. It would appear to Quentin that his daughter turned away because she was devastated by his accusations, but in reality, Maya didn't want her father to see that she wanted to burst out in laughter. This entire ordeal was one big joke to Maya. She got a sick kick out of causing chaos and finding ways to weasel out of it.

"Daddy, I feel horrible that I continue to put you in the middle of this madness between me, Precious, and Aaliyah. You don't deserve it. I thought we were passed this. Precious seemed to want us to build a real sister relationship, but Aaliyah continues to fight against that. Of course I can't fault Precious for siding with her daughter, but Daddy, you have to see that Aaliyah is lying. If it weren't for you, I would be in jail right now for attempted murder."

"Clearly Aaliyah made a mistake about..."

"No! That wasn't a mistake. She was purposely trying to pin that on me, but luckily I had an alibi in you. Then she got angry at you for telling the truth. Aaliyah knew that it wasn't me, but she didn't care. When those charges didn't stick she tried to blame her kidnapping on me when it was obvious that Arnez was responsible. You saw the damage he did to my face."

Maya's voice began to tremble as if she was fighting back tears. Then her bottom lip started to quiver. It was beginning to seem that Maya had missed her calling in life to be an award-winning actress.

"It's not my intention to upset you, Maya," Quentin said standing up. He walked over to console his daughter. "Maya, you're shaking," he continued, holding her tightly trying to calm her down.

"I don't know how much more of this I can take.

I've tried to turn my life around, but everyone wants to keep living in the past. Precious has done terrible things and Aaliyah is no angel, but they continue to throw accusations in my direction that are based on lies."

"All I want is the truth, Maya."

"I told you the truth! That night after I spoke to you on the phone, Arnez showed up at my apartment with a gun. He forced me to go with him to some house in Brooklyn. He said he was going to kill Aaliyah and set me up to take the fall. That's when I realized that he was the one that had her all this time. He wanted it to appear there was a struggle, that's when Precious showed up. Arnez ended up shooting both of them. I tried to get away, but," Maya stopped mid-sentence and broke down in tears. "If Precious would get her memory back," Maya continued between sniffles. "Then she could back up what I'm telling you. But honestly, knowing Precious she probably does remember, but is teaming up with her daughter to bring me down. They're trying to railroad me."

Maya was passionate with her story and very believable. So believable that Quentin found himself throwing all common sense out the window and taking Maya's side.

"It's gonna be alright. I'll take care of everything. I won't let you be railroaded," Quentin assured her.

"Thank you, Daddy," Maya cried in her father's face and smiled wickedly behind his back.

Chapter Eighteen

Bait

Skylar strategically placed her naked body on the sand as the waves cascaded against her skin. She knew that any minute Gabe would be showing up to begin his shift and this was the entrance he used. From the corner of her eye, Skylar could see Gabe opening the gate. She began stretching her torso, extending her legs and exposing her breasts in the most discreet, non-discreet way possible.

The glistening bronze, wet, naked body immediately caught Gabe's attention. He practically tripped over himself to get a closer look at the woman on the beach.

"Umm, excuse me, but..."

"Omigoodness! What are you doing here?!" Skylar screamed, reaching for her towel to cover herself up.

"I came to work... and I... I saw you here..." he stuttered.

"I feel so embarrassed. I need to go," Skylar said grabbing her belongings.

"Wait! You don't have to go," Gabe said putting his hand on Skylar's wrist. He hadn't been around a beautiful naked woman in so long, he wasn't about to let Skylar get away.

"I have to go. You shouldn't have seen me like this. I'm so ashamed." Skylar put her head down as if she was mortified.

"You have no reason to be ashamed. I'm so used to doing my job and following orders that I never paid attention to how beautiful you are."

"You're just saying that because you know I feel embarrassed."

"I'm saying it because it's true." Gabe stroked the side of Skylar's face. "You have some pretty skin." He then leaned over and kissed her. Skylar's initial reaction was to slap the shit out of Gabe. She wasn't expecting him to be that direct, but Skylar had a game to play and was all in. So she kissed Gabe back and threw her tongue in for good measure.

"Follow me," Gabe said taking Skylar's hand and

leading her to a cabana. Despair had left butterflies in the pit of her stomach. She dreaded what was about to go down, but Skylar wanted to get home to her son and Genesis. She was willing to do anything to make that happen, even have sex with Gabe.

"Kiss it for me," Gabe said unbuckling his pants. Skylar wanted to vomit. She was now regretting her decision, realizing she didn't fully think her plan through.

"I don't think we should be doing this."

"Why not? I can tell you attracted to me and I'm most definitely attracted to you," he said pulling Skylar close. Gabe wasn't a bad looking dude, he was somewhat cute, but he was no Genesis and Skylar didn't want to put her lips anywhere on him especially not his dick.

"I am attracted to you, but this doesn't feel right."

"You must have a man."

"I do and a son that I want to get back home to."

"Maybe I can help you with that."

"How? You wouldn't help me, but I could help you."

"Besides sucking my dick how can you help me?"

"What's more important to you, getting your dick sucked or getting paid? How long do you want to work for free?" Skylar asked.

"Who said I'm working for free?" Gabe shot back.

"Now you're the one that looks embarrassed. But you don't have to be. I know that you all haven't

been paid. I overheard some of the cooks complaining about it."

"Say what you heard is true. How can you get some money in my pocket?"

"You must not know who my man is?"

"Nope. I don't ask no questions. I do my job and that's it."

"Let's just say if you're able to get me home to my son and man, you'll be well compensated. You'll be able to get off this island and go home and take care of your own family."

"How much money are you talkin' 'bout?"

"Name your price. Whatever the amount Genesis will pay it."

Skylar had Gabe's full attention, but this time it wasn't because of her naked body. He didn't want to say it, but he was thirsty for money. His family had been blowing his phone up and all Gabe could do was hit the ignore button because he had no answers. Julio had been continuing to give him and Mario the run around. If Skylar could put some real money in his pocket, then he was willing to listen to what she had to say.

"I'll help, but I still want some pussy too," Gabe added.

"Let me call my man and I'll consider it," Skylar countered.

"Hmmm." Gabe gave Skylar a lingering stare. She could see the hunger in his eyes and it made her uneasy, but there was no turning back now. Skylar knew Gabe was greedy. He wanted the money and the pussy, but if giving him both would get Skylar off the island, she was game.

"The ball is in your court. What you 'gon do?" Skylar sounded and appeared to be in control of the situation. But she was willing to get home by any means necessary, so that meant Gabe was holding all the cards.

"I was surprised when I got your call and asked to come over. We haven't been on the best terms since that unfortunate Chantal incident," T-Roc said, as he and Supreme sat down in his den.

"I always find it humorous when you resort to calling what your wife did an incident," Supreme said picking up the handcrafted Jay Strongwater cast metal with 18-kt gold plating and Swarovski crystals framed photo of Chantal that was on the table. "Your wife killed a man and then set my daughter up to take the fall. That's much more than an incident." Supreme exhaled, shaking his head before putting the picture frame back down.

"No need to rehash the past."

"My nigga, you brought it up. But you're right. I didn't come over here to revisit what your mental and emotionally unstable wife did to my daughter.

We've moved past that. Hopefully Chantal is getting the help she needs."

"The treatment facility where she served her time was extremely beneficial and Chantal is doing much better now."

"Yo, I don't give a fuck how your wife is doing. You didn't catch the sarcasm in my voice or were you trying to get under my skin wit' that BS you just spilled... don't answer that," Supreme quickly said when T-Roc opened his mouth to respond. "Let me get to why I asked to come over before this conversation ends before we even get it started."

"I agree," T-Roc said shifting positions in his chair.

"I know that you're close to Genesis, so I'm sure you're aware of a lot of the things that's been going on recently."

"Genesis hasn't gone into great detail, but I do know that Aaliyah was missing for an extended amount of time, but is back home safely now."

"That's partially true, but she'll never be safe until everyone who was involved in the kidnapping is taken care of permanently."

"I feel you, but I'm not sure what I can do to help."

"I'm about to talk very freely with you. I know that I can because although I have a strong disdain for your wife, we have continued to do business together even without being on the best of terms, with great success."

"True indeed. The proof is in the checks we cash." T-Roc smiled.

"No doubt. So I'm positive what I'm about to discuss with you will stay between us because you have no desire to bring down our lucrative business venture."

"Great minds think alike because you're right. If I have my way, we'll continue to make money together until the day I die. Whether you want to talk to me or not." T-Roc laughed.

"Now that we got that out the way, I need your assistance," Supreme said not amused with T-Roc's money talk.

"I'll do what I can. What you need?"

"A few weeks ago, a house out in Staten Island was burned to the ground. Supposedly, Arnez was killed in that fire."

"You talkin' 'bout Arnez Douglass?"

"Yep, that Arnez."

"That man has done everything he can to make my man's life a living hell. I'm sure Genesis is happy that motherfucker is finally dead," T-Roc scoffed.

"I'm not convinced he is dead, but I've hit a dead end and need to do some further digging. That's where you come in."

"How can I help?" T-Roc was confused.

"That house was in some dummy corporation's name. After my investigator dug deeper come to find out the owner of that dummy corporation is a man by the name of Markell Simmons."

"Markell? He used to work at my record label years ago before I sold it to Sony. That's my guy."

"I already know that. I also know he was a street nigga who sold drugs and has been continuing that line of work for several years now."

"Are you sure about that?" T-Roc wasn't convinced.

"Positive. He has been a loyal customer to yo' man Genesis for a long time now."

"Are you saying that Markell gets his drugs from Genesis?"

"That's exactly what I'm saying. He also was getting his drugs from a guy named Emory. I find it odd that Arnez would be residing at a house that was owned by a man who was doing business with his enemy. So either Markell had no idea or he was working with Arnez. I'm going with the latter."

"I haven't spoken to Markell in a while, but we're still cool. He's never mentioned any dealings with Genesis, Arnez, or this Emory dude. Is Markell still getting his drugs from both Genesis and Emory?"

"No, but that's only because Emory is dead. I had to kill him when I found out he was involved with Aaliyah's kidnapping."

T-Roc's eyes widened. "Now I get what you meant about speaking freely. I had no idea murder was part of the discussion."

"Don't act so surprised. Both of us have a few murders under our belt," Supreme reminded T-Roc.

"Hey, no judgment from me. Only making a comment."

"I don't need your comments, T-Roc. What I need is for you to speak to Markell. You all go way back. So far back that when he got arrested for attempted murder, you paid his bail, got him that job at your record label and even got him a top-notch attorney who beat the case for him. He owes you a great deal."

"I see you've done your homework."

"I have. That's why I'm a little surprised you had no idea about his dealings with Genesis, Arnez, and Emory."

"Markell was a kid with no direction when I met him. He would handle some minor situations for me. He was always a bit of a hothead, but he was loyal to me. As the years went by, he grew up and moved on. We keep in touch and see each other every once in awhile. I actually ran into him a few weeks ago, but I don't know what that man got going on. His personal and professional life is none of my concern."

"Well, it's about to be your concern. I need confirmation that Arnez is dead because I don't believe he is. I also believe that there is another person working with him and Maya. I need to know who that is and I have a feeling Markell has those answers."

"Supreme, say you're right." T-Roc shrugged. "Why would Markell open up to me about it? We don't do business together."

"But we do and I'm sure you want that business to continue."

T-Roc frowned at what Supreme was suggesting. "That's sounding like a borderline threat."

"T-Roc, you know me well enough to know I don't make threats. No need to make this more complicated than what it needs to be. Like I said, Markell owes you. You kept him from doing a long bid. It's time for you to collect. We both know how convincing you can be."

"When do you need this information by?"

"Yesterday. So get on your phone and have a conversation with Markell. But have it in person. We know how much more persuasive one can be when you speak to them face to face." Supreme smiled as he got up to leave. He was determined to bring down everyone connected to Aaliyah's kidnapping, even if it meant taking down one man at a time.

Chapter Nineteen

Good Girl Gone

Maya was driving recklessly down St. Nicholas Avenue in Harlem enjoying her freedom. It was the first time in weeks that she had been able to ride solo, without a lawyer, her father, or some security lurking. Today there was no sleeked back bun for her. She had her tresses free and blowing in the spring breeze. Maya glanced at herself in the rearview mirror. When she came to a light, she pulled out her sepia lip gloss and reapplied another coat before fluffing out her hair.

"I'm back bitches!" Maya blew herself a kiss and kept driving, oblivious to everything else that was going on in the world. She had a buzz and she didn't need a blunt or a line of coke to get it. Maya was high off of her own self-inflated ego. Once she had Quentin believing her bullshit story and got the call from her attorney that the police didn't believe they had enough evidence to pursue criminal charges against her, Maya felt untouchable. It was all she needed to hear to ditch her boring good girl attire and pull out the five-inch heels.

Maya had the music blasting so loud that she could barely hear her cell ringing. She reached over to the passenger seat to retrieve her phone, but it fell on the floor. "Damn!" she smacked, leaning down to get it while turning the corner. Maya had her eyes off the wheel for only a few seconds, but when she looked back up there was a car blocking her. After a few minutes of the car not moving, Maya began blowing her horn. "Move your fuckin' car!" she screamed out of her window, but still nothing.

Fed the fuck up from waiting for the car in front of her to move and getting no response, Maya put her car in reverse to back out. But then another car pulled up from behind blocking her in. "What the hell is going on with these fuckin' drivers today!" She threw her arms up in the air and began blowing her horn again, but when the car door opened, Maya realized this was no random coincidence.

Precious and Genesis stepped out and were walking towards her dressed all in black like they were the Hollywood hood version of Mr. and Mrs.

Smith. "Not these two motherfuckers," she mumbled. Maya started weighing her options and decided to kick off her heels and make a run for it. Then she noticed two big, black, burly motherfuckers stepping out the car that was blocking her from the front. "Where is security when you need them." Maya shook her head.

Maya's head was spinning trying to come up with a quick getaway scheme. She rolled up the window as if that would buy her some time, but it didn't. A few seconds later Precious was looking down knocking on her window.

"Get out the car, Maya. You can either get out voluntarily or we can pull you out." Precious stood with her arms folded, making it clear she was not moving.

"I'm not getting out of my car. You and your cronies need to get the hell outta here," Maya barked.

"No problem. We can do this the hard way. Hand me your gun," Precious ordered one of her henchmans. He handed her his weapon and Precious aimed it right at the glass directly to Maya's face. "Are you ready to die in broad daylight with your brain splattered in your car? If so, say the word. I'll be more than happy to put you out of your misery."

Maya wasn't sure what she was more afraid of. The fact that she knew Precious would pull the trigger or what she had planned for her once they got her out the car. Precious then gazed down at her watch. "The clock is ticking."

"Don't shoot her," Genesis whispered in Precious's ear. "I need to find out what she knows about Talisa and Skylar."

"I got this." Precious put up her hand to shoo Genesis away.

Maya bit down on her lip as anxiety kicked in wondering what words were exchanged between Precious and Genesis. Unable to help herself, Maya rolled down her window halfway, but that was the only opening Precious needed. Before Maya could say a word, Precious had reached inside the window and had Maya by the throat trying to drag her ass out her seat.

Maya was frantically gasping for air and flopping her arms to break free of Precious's grasp. She then fidgeted with the power windows, but when it started rolling up, Precious maintained her grip. Maya then had the bright idea to push the panic button on her car key, but even with the ear-piercing car alarm ringing in the Harlem air, Precious would not let go.

Genesis noticed everyone stopping in the street and looking out their apartment windows to see what was going on. A small crowd began to gather to get a closer look at the commotion going on. "Let's go! Someone is going to call 911 any minute if they haven't already and the police will be showing up. Even worse, people are going to start recording us on their cell phones and posting it to YouTube," Genesis told Precious.

Precious knew that Genesis was absolutely right, but it felt so good watching Maya die right in front of her face. Her eyes were starting to roll around in her head as she was losing the battle to breathe. Maya was now so weak, she had given up clawing her way to freedom.

"Fine!" Precious sighed, grudgingly releasing Maya's neck. "Watch your back, lil' sister 'cause this is far from over. I'll be seeing you again real soon.

While walking back to their cars, Precious glanced back to see Maya still struggling to catch her breath. She was furious she had been unable to finish choking the life out of Maya, but under the circumstances she had no choice but to bail.

"This was a bust," Genesis moaned as their driver pulled off.

"Maybe a bust for you, but that right there was better than having sex for me," Precious boasted. "Watching the life drain out of Maya's eyes was almost the perfect aphrodisiac. Unfortunately, she didn't die, but we'll be able to take care of that soon enough."

"I thought we had an understanding, Precious. You wouldn't—"

"I know... I know," Precious interrupted Genesis. "I wouldn't kill Maya until after you got the information you needed regarding your wife and Skylar. I got you."

"I couldn't tell based on what just took place a few minutes ago."

"Maya's still alive isn't she," Precious snarled.

"Yeah, because Maya came up with the smart idea to have her car alarm go off."

"No one ever said my demonic sister wasn't crafty, but hey so is the devil." Precious shrugged.

"Boy oh boy, I see why you have all the men in your life going crazy. You are a piece of work, Precious," Genesis said before answering his phone. "Hello."

"Genesis, it's me... Skylar."

"Skylar! Baby, where are you?"

Precious sat up in her seat when she realized Genesis was speaking to Skylar. Even though she knew it wasn't her fault that Skylar was taken, Precious couldn't shake a sense a guilt that she was kidnapped on her watch.

"Where are you, Skylar?" Genesis asked again.

"I'm not sure. On some remote island, but I'm coming home. I just need you to pay this man."

"Okay, how much? Just tell me the price."

"I'm not sure yet. We're negotiating that right now. But he let me use his phone so I could let you know that I'm okay. Arnez is the one who's behind this, but this man is going to help me get home."

"Put the man on the phone," Genesis demanded. There was a brief pause.

"He doesn't want to speak to you. He said he'll let me call you again after we work everything out. I love you."

"I love you, too. Do you..." The phone went dead before Genesis could finish his sentence. "She's alive. Skylar's alive." Genesis sat back in relief.

"This means we don't have to keep Maya alive. We don't need her." Precious's tone was dripping with enthusiasm.

"I understand your hatred for Maya, but can we not make it about her for one second. Is that asking too much?"

"You're right. I apologize, Genesis. We should be celebrating that you spoke to Skylar and she's alive. What did she say?"

"That she was coming home."

"Really... when?"

"I couldn't get many details from her. I got the feeling that someone was right there in her face listening to everything she said. What I do know is that she's on some remote island."

"An island... that's interesting. But that could be anywhere."

"Exactly. She also said that Arnez is the one that had her kidnapped."

"She told you that."

"We pretty much knew it, but now that we have confirmation from Skylar it makes me believe more than ever that what he said about Talisa is true... that she's alive."

"Genesis, that would be a beautiful thing, but if Talisa comes home, what does that mean for your relationship with Skylar?"

"I love Skylar and her son, but Talisa is my wife, the love of my life. No other woman could ever come before that."

"I get it. Trust me, I know exactly what you mean," Precious said, gazing out the window thinking about the man she considered to be the love of her life too.

Chapter Twenty

Confessions

"Aaliyah, it's so good to see you. Give your old man a hug," Supreme said, squeezing his daughter tightly.

"It's good to see you too, Daddy."

"You've been on the go ever since they released you from the hospital. Hope you not moving too fast. Maybe you need to slow down."

"I'm good. I actually had a follow up with my doctor the other day and he said I'm recovering nicely," she beamed.

"That's good to hear. You look beautiful, but you always do just like your mother."

"Thanks, Daddy. You always make me feel so special."

"Because you are and don't ever forget it. If a man doesn't let you know how special you are then he ain't the one. I'm sitting outside by the pool. Come join me," Supreme said as Aaliyah followed him outside. "Do you want me to have Elena bring you something to drink or eat?"

"No, I'm good. Plus, I'm meeting Dale for an early dinner when I leave here."

"Okay, well I better enjoy the time I'm spending with you since you'll have to leave soon."

"No rush. It's nice being here with you. Sitting outside. It's such a beautiful day. Perfect to be relaxing by the pool."

"I agree."

"Dad, you don't feel lonely being in this humongous house by yourself? Xavier has been staying with mom and soon he'll be going off to college. Are you going to stay here when he leaves or are you going back to your house in LA?"

"I have a few things I need to resolve here, so I won't be going back to LA anytime soon. This estate is rather large for a bachelor," Supreme commented looking around. "But it's hard to let go. I still remember when you were a little girl and we celebrated Christmas here. So many memories."

"Memories of you and Mom. I know you call yourself a bachelor, but I kinda now you still love Mom."

"Precious is a married woman."

"On paper only. You know how much I love Nico."

"And you should, he's your father. It took me so many years to accept that it was okay for you to love both of us. For so long in my stubborn head, I thought if you loved Nico, it meant that you couldn't love me too. Thank God, good sense finally kicked in." Supreme laughed. "It's true, you're never too old to learn."

"I'm so lucky to have you, Daddy."

"I'm the lucky one." He smiled.

"But like I was saying, I love Nico very much and I know how much he loves my mom. I also knew that them getting married wasn't going to last, because the moment my mother got her memory back she would come running to you. Like I predicated, that's what happened."

"Your mother is an amazing woman, albeit an extremely complicated one. As much as I love her, I think she might be better off with Nico."

"Daddy, I never thought I would ever hear you say that! How can you say that? You're the love of mother's life and I know she's yours."

"If only life was that simple. Many would still consider me to be a relatively young man in his prime, but I've experienced more than most men have in their 60s, 70s, and 80s. The point is, I might still look young, but my mind feels like it's a hundred years old. Your mother has worn me out." Supreme chuckled. "I can't keep up with her shenanigans at this point in my life. Too tired, baby girl." Supreme playfully squeezed Aaliyah's arm.

"Oh, Daddy."

"Oh, Daddy, nothing. As the years have gone by, I've learned that a peace of mind is priceless. It's rare with all the craziness that goes on in life, so when you can grab a piece of it, you better hold on tight."

"Even if that means being without the one you love? That's a huge sacrifice."

"What do you know about sacrificing? You haven't been in love before."

"I think I'm in love with Dale. I could see myself spending the rest of my life with him," Aaliyah stated.

Supreme lifted up his glass and took a sip of his drink. Aaliyah couldn't get a read on what he was thinking because her father had always been excellent at disguising his true feelings. Unless he voluntarily shared his thoughts it would remain a mystery. It was one of the qualities that made him so alluring to people.

"Only time will tell if you're truly in love with Dale. But enjoy the moment. Falling in love is probably the best part of the process." He grinned as if reminiscing about when he first fell in love.

"That wasn't the answer I was expecting to hear."

"What did you think I would say?"

"I don't know. Maybe warn me to stay away from him or say he wasn't good enough. You know those

things parents typically say to their kids when their significant other isn't an ideal mate."

"I wouldn't do that to you even if I felt that way because it doesn't work. My parents, especially your grandmother, never wanted me to marry your mother. I was this young, rich, superstar rapper and they didn't understand with all of my options, why I wanted to marry Precious Cummings. The answer was simple to me though."

"Which was?" Aaliyah asked with eager curiosity.

"For me, it didn't get no better than her. She was the craziest, funniest, realest and most loving woman I had ever met. Precious fit me, like this," Supreme said, clasping his fingers between each other. "So no matter what my parents said, they weren't going to stop me from marrying her. If you wanna be with Dale, there is nothing I can say to stop you either."

"You really are wise, Daddy."

"Don't sound so surprised. I've lived a very colorful life and I ain't done yet."

"You know what I find most intriguing about you?"

"What's that?"

"I can sit here and discuss Dale, how much I love him and you listen so intently. Showing no signs that you're against our relationship."

"Why would I be?"

"Maybe because you're the one who killed his brother Emory."

"Oh… that." Supreme spoke indifferently almost callous.

"Yeah, that! Were you ever planning on telling me that it was you? When Dale was supposed to come see me at the hospital, I told you he couldn't make it because he found out his brother was murdered and how distraught he was. You said nothing to me!" Aaliyah seemed ready to spit fire.

"What was I supposed to say?"

"That you were responsible for my boyfriend's brother's death," she ridiculed, rolling her eyes in frustration.

"Aaliyah, what good would that have done?"

"For one, not being blindsided when I heard it from Amir. I was completely taken off guard."

"I apologize for that. Amir should've kept that information to himself. He was told during a private business meeting with the family while you and your mother were missing. He should know better then to go running off at the mouth," Supreme said dismayed.

"He figured that you had already told me since I'm your daughter."

"It wasn't his business to figure anything. Amir is young though, he's still learning how these things work."

"That's all you have to say? What about you killing Emory?" Aaliyah said becoming more upset.

"What about it? I did what I had to do. He was working with Arnez and Maya. He was also fuckin' her, excuse my language, and she had his mind all messed up. I did that boy a favor by killing him. Can you imagine what yo' mother would've done if she found out."

"I'm still having a hard time believing that," Aaliyah sighed.

"Well believe it. Emory was a snake. He knew Dale was in a relationship with you, but decided to get in bed with your enemy. What type of brother does that? I had no choice but to kill Emory. I would've killed Arnez too, but he knew where you and your mother was being held so I let him live, but now it's time for him to die too," Supreme said matter of factly.

"Wow!"

"Wow, what?"

"Call me naïve, but besides my brother, I thought you were the only other person in our family that wasn't a cold-blooded killer."

"I'll never apologize for doing whatever needs to be done to protect my family. I would kill anybody that tried to hurt you, your brother, or your mother. You're my family and I'll kill for mine without giving it a second thought."

"Don't you think Dale is going to feel the same way when he finds out that you killed his brother because that's his family."

"See, that right there is why I didn't want you to know that I was the one who killed Emory. I never wanted to put you in a position where you felt you had to choose between your father or the man that you love. I know firsthand that the heart has a mind and a voice of its own."

"I just don't know if I can keep this secret to myself. I feel like I'm lying to Dale when I know the truth. I see how this is eating him up."

"Do you think telling him that your father is the one who killed his brother will make him feel any better? It won't bring Emory back... he's still dead."

"If Dale knows all the facts then he'll have to understand why you did what you did. You were protecting me."

"Let me tell you something baby girl. When someone is your family and you truly love them, they can do the most despicable things in the world and you'll always try to find a way to justify their actions because you love them. Do you believe that Dale loves you more than his dead brother? Because that is what it would take for him to forgive me for protecting you."

Aaliyah wanted to believe that Dale loved her more, but if she was being honest with herself, she wasn't sure. For so long it was always them against the world. Their bond was almost unbreakable. Aaliyah finally had a man in her life that she believed fit her. The way her dad said her mother fit him. She wasn't willing to take a gamble of losing Dale because of his corrupt brother.

Chapter Twenty-One

Empty Lies

"Daddy, please help me," Maya cried out when Quentin opened the door.

"Maya, what happened to you? Come sit down," he said taking her hand. Maya was disheveled with ligature marks around her neck.

"Precious happened to me. I want her arrested."

"Slow down. Why do you want Precious arrested?"

"Because she just tried to kill me in broad daylight. You see these marks around my neck. Precious did this. Her and her cronies, which included Genesis by the way, blocked my car in and tried to snatch me up in the middle of Harlem. She's crazy, Daddy. The only way to stop her is to go to the police and have her arrested," Maya wailed.

"Precious has been through a lot. Having your sister arrested isn't the answer," Quentin said calmly.

"How can you say that?! She tried to kill me! She's out of her mind. If she's not put in jail, next time she might succeed and I can end up dead."

"Maya, there won't be a next time. I'm going to talk to Precious right now. I'ma have my driver take you to my house in Alpine. You'll be safe there. Don't speak to anyone especially the police. Do you understand me?"

"I understand. But if you can't reign Precious in, I will be calling Detective Garcia to have charges brought against her for assault. I'm not gonna live my life being terrorized by my crazy ass sister."

"Let me handle Precious, you just lay low for a few days while I get things under control. All of this acrimony has to come to an end. If it takes the last breath in my body, there will be peace between you and your sister," Quentin promised.

When T-Roc arrived at Markell's full floor penthouse duplex loft on West 16th Street, he was impressed.

He took a private key lock elevator up to a modern day oasis. The rooftop deck had views of The Empire State building with a hot tub, outdoor shower, linear glass fire pit, multiple seating and dining areas with a garden. It could easily accommodate fifty people with no problem.

The inside had a Control4 Smart Home System, open kitchen with Viking, Subzero and Miele appliances including a wine storage. There was a Solarban shade system installed for privacy and the bedrooms had a balcony accessible by both rooms.

"You up in here living like a king." T-Roc smiled.

"Only keeping up with you or at least trying. I ain't quite there yet," Markell replied.

"It looks like you on the way. Maybe I need to dabble into whatever business you doing."

"Nah, you good over there. You've been rich since I was taking the train and I ain't took the train in a long time. That means you been getting money forever," Markell joked.

"You might be right, but I'm still proud of you. You doing real good for yourself and I like that."

"Appreciate it. It's no secret I always looked up to you. Not only were you a mentor, you had my back when everyone else had turned theirs on me."

"You were a kid that needed some guidance. It must've worked 'cause look at you now," T-Roc said putting his hands up, acknowledging how good Markell was living. "So do you plan on telling your mentor how you've been able to obtain all this?"

T-Roc watched as Markell gave a nervous laugh, poured himself another drink before walking over to the expansive living room and turning the volume way up on the television. Markell then came back over to where T-Roc was standing.

"Open your shirt," Markell demanded.

"Excuse me?" T-Roc raised an eyebrow with a what the fuck is going on stare.

"Open your shirt. I wanna see if you wearing a wire."

"Hold up. You think I'm an informant? Is you fuckin' crazy! Nigga you know me."

"Yeah, I also know you got mad skeletons in yo' closet. Maybe all the dirt you done came back to bite you in the ass and to save yo'self, you made a deal wit' the Feds."

"No disrespect, Markell, but if I had to make a deal wit' the Feds, I have much bigger fish I could feed them than you."

"Then why out the fuckin' blue do you reach out to me, tryna come to my home and asking all these questions about how I'm making my money? Why the fuck do you care? And don't give me that lame excuse about wanting to make money wit' me, 'cause we all know you already a rich nigga," Markell barked. "If you ain't an informant, then what's really going on?"

"Have a seat. But before you do, can you turn down that fuckin' tv."

T-Roc presumed an indirect approach wasn't

working with Markell. So he was going to lay his cards on the table in an attempt to get the information he needed.

"T-Roc, don't be bullshitting me, man. We go too far back for that," Markell said, sitting across from him.

"Exactly. That's why I'm insulted you would come at me like that."

"You should understand where I'm coming from. We both know how this game goes. People are quick to turn on you to fit they own agenda."

"True... true. I'll admit my approach could've been more forthcoming. We go way back and based off that, I should've played it straight with you."

Markell nodded his head cosigning on what T-Roc said. "Now that we got all that established. Tell me what's really going on.

"What's your relationship with a dude named Arnez Douglass?"

"I don't know an Arnez," Markell said flatly.

"Oh really. So you gon' just sit there, look me in the face and tell me a lie? I guess all that shit you was spitting at me was all lies."

Markell hung his head down and began breathing hard. He wasn't here for the conversation T-Roc was pushing to have. "Like I said, I don't know Arnez."

"Then why was he staying at your house in Staten Island? And don't tell me you don't own a house in Staten Island. I already know you have it in some dummy company's name, but you are the owner of that so what gives."

"Damn! You fucked me up with that. But you always been thorough so I shouldn't be surprised."

"Then are you ready to tell me the truth?" T-Roc pressed.

"Okay, so I do know Arnez. What's that to you?"

"Honestly, it don't mean shit to me. I could give two fucks about that man, but someone that I do a lot of business with, does care. So I'll ask you again, what's your relationship with Arnez?"

"Do you have beef wit' him?" Markell wanted to know before answering.

"Nah, I told you I don't have any issues wit' that man. But this ain't about me and it shouldn't be about you either."

"Point taken."

"Good. Now answer my question." T-Roc had become vexed battling to get the information he needed from Markell. But he knew this was important to Supreme, so he wanted to deliver and it just wasn't because they made a lot of money together. T-Roc would never admit it out loud, but he felt guilty about what Chantal did to not only his daughter, but also to Aaliyah and Precious. This was his way of trying to make things right."

Markell let out a heavy sigh before giving up the goods. "At one point I used to dip and dabble in stocks. I was actually great at it. I made some investments for Arnez. Nothing too heavy, but he was impressed.

One day he asked me did I want to make some real money. So I was like what you mean by some real money. Once he broke down the numbers, I decided to give dude a try."

"What did Arnez need for you to do in order for you to collect?" T-Roc could see that Markell was hesitating to continue. "Do I need to remind you if it wasn't for me, you'd be doing twenty to life right now."

"Damn, T-Roc, you takin' it there?" Markell frowned. "You must be making a lot of money wit' this business associate of yours to be going this hard."

"It's not just about money. But on the real, I shouldn't have to jump through all these hoops for you to tell me what the fuck you know." T-Roc's jaw flinched. "I've done more than just keep you from spending the rest of your life caged up like an animal. We both know that."

"He fronted the money so I could start buying drugs from a dude named Genesis."

"How long have you been buying from Genesis?"

"A few years now, but recently I've been dealing with his son. They having problems with their operation, but Arnez has had that in the works for a very long time."

"Why is that?" T-Roc asked not letting Markell know that not only was Genesis a good friend of his, but he was well aware of the history between him and Arnez. T-Roc wanted to see how forthcoming Markell was being.

"I like Genesis. He's always done above the

board business with me, but Arnez can't stand the nigga. He's been meticulous with his plot to bring him down which includes his drug operation. Like I said, I like the dude, but my money comes from Arnez so that's where my alliance is."

"Is Arnez still alive?"

Markell hesitated again, but once he started talking, there was no holding him back. "Yep, he's alive but he in bad shape." Markell shook his head. "This chick he was dealing with did a number on him."

"What's the chick's name?"

"Not sure. Arnez didn't tell me."

"Where is Arnez now... and don't bullshit me, Markell."

"He's staying in another house that I own, trying to recuperate. Like I said, he's pretty fucked up. That chick left him for dead."

"I see. What about Emory... does Arnez have you getting your drugs from him too?"

"Emory... you know all my business."

"Not all, but enough. So tell me about your dealings with Emory."

"I was getting drugs from him too but ummm, he's dead."

"Really. How do you know that?"

"Arnez told me. He even told me that the nigga Supreme did it. I ain't talkin' 'bout no street nigga named Supreme, I'm talkin' 'bout 'The' Supreme. Superstar rapper Supreme. Can you believe that shit." Markell smiled.

"Nah, I can't," T-Roc said although he already knew. He was pleased that Markell was being so open with him. That made him confident to ask his next question. "Will you give me the address where Arnez is staying?"

"I don't know, T-Roc. I don't feel comfortable doing that."

"Why not?"

"'Cause I already know ain't nothing good gon' come from it."

"You probably right. But from what you told me, Arnez is gonna be out of commission for the foreseeable future. So he won't be much help to your pockets. Are you sure you wanna protect a cat that has no loyalty to anyone but himself?"

Markell pulled out a pen and on the back of a card he wrote down the address. "Arnez has around the clock care so he won't be alone. Two nurses rotate shifts. Try not to hurt them too 'cause they're really nice ladies."

"Thanks for the heads up," T-Roc said, shaking Markell's hand. "Don't be a stranger. Now that you'll no longer be doing business with Arnez, maybe I can be of some assistance. Think about it."

"Will do," Markell replied, walking T-Roc to the door.

From the moment after Markell closed the door to before he even made it to his car, T-Roc hit up Supreme. "I got that info you need."

Chapter Twenty-Two

Coming Home

"Each time keeps getting better and better," Gabe grinned while zipping up his pants.

Skylar grabbed her kimono cover up and put it on. Gabe had been demanding sex daily since her phone call to Genesis. She was starting to feel like his sex slave. Instead of plotting on how to get back home she was starting to plot how to kill Gabe.

"This was the last time. Obviously you have no intention of helping me get off this island, so I'm done fucking you."

"I thought you were enjoying it as much as I was," Gabe said rubbing his fingers across Skylar's lips.

"Get your hands off of me," she snapped, slapping them away. "Don't ever touch me again."

"Calm down, sexy. No need to be hostile."

"You've wasted my time. I'm sure Mario or better yet Julio would be more than happy to take me up on my offer. Everybody knows that things are real dry around here. Ain't no money coming in. I think I'll go have a conversation with them right now."

"Hold up sexy lady!" Gabe grabbed Skylar's arm as she was storming out.

"Didn't I tell you not to ever touch me again."

"Cool," Gabe said putting his hands up and backing off. "No need to run off to Mario or Julio. If you would've gave me a second, I could've told you that I've already made arrangements for you to get off the island."

"When?"

"Friday."

"This Friday?"

"Yep, all you have to do is call your boyfriend to set shit up."

"Don't play with me, Gabe."

"Listen, I'm enjoying smashin', you sexy as fuck but you right, a nigga's pockets is hurtin' right now. I need that money more than I need yo' pussy."

"Good! So give me your phone. I need to call my man so I can get the hell off this island."

"I tell you what. You throw extra few thousands in there, you can take Talisa with you too."

"That won't be necessary."

"Ya'll seemed close. I thought that was your homegirl."

"You thought wrong. Talisa is sweet, but there's no place for her back in New York. Her life is here now, on this island. Now give me your phone."

"I think this is the most beautiful I've ever seen you look," Dale said as he and Aaliyah danced in the moonlight surrounded by seven pillar candles with floral centerpieces, rose petals, and a pianist playing classical love songs.

"I'm glad you like it." Aaliyah twirled around playfully showcasing her look from head to toe. She was stunning in an ivory low cut gown with a thigh high split in the front and lace detail. Paired with five inch Jimmy Choo crystal covered peep toe pumps with a delicate buckled ankle strap.

"I can only think of one more thing that would make you look even more perfect."

"Oh really? All of this isn't perfect enough for you," Aaliyah teased.

Dale took Aaliyah's hand and pulled her close as if performing a ballroom dance. He looked equally as stunning in a light blue signature Tom Ford "O'Connor" base trim suit in solid silk. "I want you to be my wife." Dale stated with his eyes piercing deeply into hers.

"What type of proposal is that? What happened to bended knee, glimmering diamond... you know all that good stuff that girls like." Aaliyah giggled.

"Say no more." Dale stepped away from Aaliyah and got down on bended knee. He reached in his pocket pulling out a classic Harry Winston, radiant cut, fancy yellow, 9.48 carat diamond, with brilliant diamond side stones, set in platinum and 18k yellow gold.

Aaliyah stood covering her mouth. She was in complete shock. "I was kidding," she said with her hand trembling.

"Why are you shaking?" Dale asked stroking her hand.

"Because I wasn't expecting this."

"Does that mean you don't want to be my wife?"

"Of course I want to be your wife. The question is, are you sure you want me to be your wife." She laughed nervously. "We both know I'm not the easiest person to deal with," Aaliyah remarked, as a tear began to trickle down her face.

"I know and I wouldn't have it any other way. With my brother being taken away from me so suddenly, I realize how important it is to be with the person you love and that person is you. I want to spend the rest of my life with you. Aaliyah Mills Carter, will you marry me?"

"Yes! Yes! Yes! Nothing would make me happier,"

Aaliyah beamed as Dale slid the ring on her finger.

Aaliyah latched onto Dale tightly as he literally swept her off her feet. She had found the man she envisioned being with forever and she now felt her life was like a fairytale.

"What did he say?" Nico questioned when Genesis got off the phone with their drug connect.

"Not what I wanted to hear. He said our shipment is going to be delayed by another week."

"You gotta be fuckin' kidding me! This shit is getting ridiculous. It has never taken this long for us to get product before," Nico scoffed.

"I agree. Something about this shit don't feel right, but I can't put my finger on it," Genesis said.

"Me neither. Maybe it's time we start looking for a new connect. I have to go to Miami. I can definitely speak with a couple of my people there."

"Is your Miami trip strictly business or something else," Genesis inquired.

"One of my guys has a lead on Angel. I'm going there tonight."

"Glad to hear that. You already got one daughter back, it'd be great if that number can be two."

"That would be a beautiful thing. I've already missed out on over twenty years, I don't wanna miss another day."

"Keep yo' head up. I think it's gonna work out for you, my man. Have you told Aaliyah about her sister yet?"

"No. I was trying to find a time to sit down and tell her, but it's almost impossible to get a hold of her. She's always with that boyfriend of hers, Dale."

"I guess they're getting serious."

"Seems that way. I remember being her age. I was in love with her mother."

"And you still are." Genesis laughed.

"Don't remind me." Nico frowned. "But as soon as I get back from Miami, I'm telling Aaliyah about Angel. If things work out the way I hope, the three of us will be sitting down for dinner where I can formally introduce them. How lucky am I to have two beautiful daughters," Nico stated proudly.

"Lucky indeed." Genesis nodded before hearing his phone ring. "Hold on for a second. Let me get this call."

"No, you take it. I have to handle some things before I catch my flight. I'll call you when I get to Miami," Nico said, heading out.

"Cool!" Genesis called out before answering his phone. "Hello."

"Genesis, it's me Skylar."

"It's good to hear your voice again. What took so long for you to call me again? I thought something happened to you."

"No, I'm okay. Things have been moving a lot

slower than I hoped, but everything is good now. If you're willing to pay then I'll be back in your arms by Friday."

"Of course I'll pay. I don't care what the amount is."

"I was hoping you would say that. I'ma text you over the account information to wire the money and where you can pick me up."

"Okay, when should I expect the text?"

"As soon as we get off the phone."

"How do we know that he's going to let you go after we pay him?"

"You're going to pay him half now and then the other half when I call and let you know I'm back in New York safely."

"Sounds good. I'll be waiting for that text."

"I can't wait to see you. Please let Brandon know his mommy will be home soon."

"I will."

"Love you… see you soon. Bye."

"Skylar wait!" Genesis yelled out before she hung up.

"Yes, what is it, baby?"

"Is there anybody else on the island with you?"

"Anybody else, like who? You mean besides the guards and the staff working on the island?"

"Yes. You know someone else being held hostage besides you?"

"No, there's no one else. Why, is someone else supposed to be here besides me?"

"Nah, I was just curious."

"Oh, I have to go. I'll see you soon. Love you."

"I love you, too." Genesis hung up disappointed. He was elated that Skylar would finally be coming home to not only him, but also her family. At the same time he was devastated that Talisa wouldn't be coming home with her.

Chapter Twenty-Three

Unstoppable

"Mother, I wanted you to be the first to know." Aaliyah scooted on the couch, moving closer to Precious.

"The first to know what? Oh my goodness are you pregnant?!" Precious gasped.

"No." Aaliyah laughed. "At least not yet. But I'll be a married woman soon, so you never know," Aaliyah said with a wide smile, showing off the rock Dale put on her finger.

Precious grabbed Aaliyah's hand. "It's gorgeous! You're engaged! I can't believe it!" she gushed.

"Yes! Dale and I are getting married."

"You're marrying Dale!" Xavier exclaimed, coming into the living room.

"Xavier, I didn't realize you were home," Aaliyah said, surprised to see her brother.

"You probably should've checked with Mom before sharing your news. I mean, I am living here," he cracked.

"I know, but I keep forgetting. Please don't say anything to Dad. I want to tell him first," Aaliyah told her brother.

"I won't, but are you sure Dale is the guy you want to spend the rest of your life with? I always assumed you and Amir would get back together," Xavier said, coming closer to examine his sister's ring. "Can't lie, dude has great taste. This ring is pricey yet classy." Xavier winked his eye with approval.

"It is gorgeous," Precious agreed. "I have a great idea. We should have a family dinner so you can announce your engagement."

"Umm, who would we invite? Dad and Nico... that would be pleasant," Xavier said sarcastically. "Oh and are either one of you speaking to grandfather or is he still on you all's shit list."

"Watch your mouth, Xavier!" Precious warned.

"It's true. Grandfather loves both of you so much, but you all cut him off like it's nothing. I guess we can invite Genesis, since he gets along with everybody. But do we invite Amir too or would that be uncomfortable for you, big sis?"

"Shut up, Xavier!" Aaliyah snapped. "Maybe this

dinner thing isn't a good idea, Mom." Aaliyah folded her arms, mad because she was actually looking forward to the family soiree.

"I think we should move forward. I'll call Nico and Supreme. They can get along for a couple hours. I'm also going to invite Quentin." Precious sighed. "I know we said we weren't dealing with him because of his relationship with Maya, but your brother is right. Quentin loves us, especially you, Aaliyah, so much. He would be crushed if he wasn't a part of your engagement party."

"You're right and I do miss him," Aaliyah admitted.

"Your engagement announcement will bring about some much needed celebrating and healing on all of our part. I'm looking forward to planning everything."

"How fast can you put it together?" Aaliyah wanted to know.

"It shouldn't take that long. Why? Are you in some kind of rush?"

"Well Dale has to go to Miami in a few days and he's going to be gone for awhile. I plan on joining him after I take care of some things here. Daddy also left me a message saying he was going out of town, I think tomorrow."

"Oh wow. I only need a couple of days to put together something nice. I'll have it at some fancy restaurant and let them do all the work. All we have to do is show up and look fabulous, my love," Precious beamed giving Aaliyah a hug. "Let me get Nico on the phone. I'm sure he can prolong his trip for a few days. I'm thinking Saturday will be the perfect."

"Thank you, Mom, for doing this. You're the best." She squeezed Precious even tighter.

"It's my pleasure. My baby girl is getting married. You're going to have the most beautiful wedding ever. I promise."

"Where are you rushing off to?" Talisa asked Skylar when she came in from swimming. "You've been disappearing a lot lately," she said wrapping a towel around her wet hair.

"I found this spot on the beach that's really tranquil. I've been going there and reading a book one of the cooks gave me," Skylar lied.

"Oh that's nice. I'm glad you're finding some peace within this nightmare. Does that mean you've given up on trying to find a way for us to escape this island?"

"For now."

"I have to admit, I'm disappointed. You were giving me hope that I would finally make it home to my husband and son. I guess it's time for me to give up on that dream." Talisa turned away putting her head down to stop herself from crying.

"Well, I have to go. My little place of peace is waiting for me and I really want to see what's going to happen next in this book."

"That's fine. Go 'head. I'll see you back here for dinner," Talisa stated.

"Of course. One good thing about this place, the food is excellent."

"So true. Enjoy your book. I'll see you later on." Talisa gave a slight wave goodbye.

"Bye, see you then." Skylar smiled, lying some more. Today she was going back home to Genesis and this was the last time she ever planned on seeing Talisa again.

"I wasn't sure if you were home. I hope you don't mind me stopping by unannounced," Amir said when Justina let him in.

"You know you're always welcomed over here. My mom just left a few minutes ago. She would've loved to see you."

"How is your mom doing?"

"Better... much better. But I'm sure you didn't come over to talk about my mom. So what brings you by?"

"I wanted to see if you would like to attend a dinner with me on Saturday."

"A dinner.... what sort of dinner and who is it for?"

"It's more like an engagement party."

"Engagement... who's getting married?" Justina was puzzled.

"Aaliyah. She just got engaged to Dale."

"Are you serious?"

"Yep. Precious called me yesterday to invite me to come."

"This must be awkward for you being that at one time you and Aaliyah were very much in love."

"Aaliyah and I had our shot. We tried and it didn't work. No love lost. We're still friends just the way we started off."

"It still must hurt just a little."

"I'm good. I've had another relationship since we broke up and she's been with Dale for a minute now, so this engagement isn't shocking for me. I'm actually really glad for her. Aaliyah's been through a lot. She deserves some happiness."

"I can't disagree with you about that. She does deserve some happiness and that's why I have to decline your dinner invite." Justina laughed. "I'm positive I'm one of the last people she wants showing up at her engagement party."

"That's where you're wrong. I cleared it with both Precious and Aaliyah."

"And they said yes?" Justina was shocked.

"Precious said if it was cool with Aaliyah, it was fine with her. Aaliyah thought it was a good idea. She said she's the happiest she's ever been in her life and wants to put the past behind her."

"Wow, I don't know what to say."

"Say you'll come. This could be a new beginning for all of us," Amir said.

"Okay. I'll come with you to the dinner. Not only do I have to find something to wear, I have to figure out what to get Aaliyah for an engagement gift."

"How about we go together to get Aaliyah's gift because I could use your help." Amir laughed.

"Sounds like a plan. What you got going on today?" Justina questioned.

"Shopping on Fifth Avenue?"

"That's right. Let me grab my purse and keys then we're out of here."

Amir smiled as Justina grabbed his arm and they headed out the door. It was like old times when they were teenagers. It felt easy and comfortable being around his high school sweetheart. Except Justina was no longer the cute yet awkward girlfriend. She had grown into a drop dead beautiful woman, but her sweetness was still intact.

Chapter Twenty-Four

I Love You Daddy

Genesis was becoming anxious as he waited to hear from Skylar. He had already paid the first half of the money and at any minute, she was supposed to arrive back safely in New York and call, letting him know it was okay to send the remaining half. He knew there was always a chance something could go wrong. That's why Genesis chose not to let anyone know what was going on, especially not Skylar's son and Mom. He didn't want to bring them any more unnecessary pain.

Pacing the floor was starting to drive Genesis crazy. When he was ready to sit down, his cell rang. "Hello!" he answered without even checking the number.

"Baby, it's me," Skylar said in a gentle, sugary sweet voice.

"Did everything go smoothly... are you straight?"

"Everything went perfect. I'm in a taxi now headed to you so you can go ahead and send the rest of the money."

"Thank God it all worked out. I won't even pretend that I wasn't scared."

"I was scared too but I'm coming home. Go ahead and make the payment. I'm gonna call my mom. I'll see you shortly. I love you so much, Genesis."

"I love you too, baby. See you soon."

"I'm finally going home," Skylar closed her eyes and said out loud after hanging up with Genesis. She had accomplished what seemed like the impossible. Yes, she had to basically prostitute herself out to Gabe and yes, she deceived Talisa and left her behind, but Skylar had no regrets. She would now be with the man that she loved and Talisa would remain a ghost. Skylar reasoned that it was best for everyone involved that Genesis's wife remain dead.

When Supreme arrived to the colonial brick house on the tree lined street, no one would guess that a deranged killer was recuperating behind the closed doors. The Honda Accord that T-Roc said would be parked in the driveway was there which meant Arnez's home attendant was in the house too.

Supreme rang the doorbell and a few seconds later an older lady with a sweet disposition opened the door. "Can I help you?" she asked Supreme who had the appearance of a businessman in a tailored three piece suit and silk tie.

"Mrs. Harris, correct?"

"Yes, I'm Mrs. Harris. Do I know you?"

"No, you don't. But I know your husband, Bernard, who works at a warehouse. You have two daughters and a son who recently had your first grandchild."

"How do you know all that about me?" the lady questioned with her face encompassed in fear.

"No need to be afraid if you take this." Supreme held out a large envelope full of one hundred dollar bills. "Leave now and never tell anyone you ever saw me. You'll be able to provide a better life for you and your family."

"If I don't take it?" she asked meekly.

"Then that fear you have on your face is justified. Neither one of us wants that. So take the money and go."

Mrs. Harris ran back in the house and hastily grabbed her purse and other belongings before coming back out. "I ain't seen nothing or heard nothing," she said taking the envelope from Supreme.

"Good. Now where is Arnez?"

"Upstairs in the bedroom at the end of the hall. He's asleep, but should be waking up soon."

"No worries. I know how to wake him up. Oh, and Mrs. Harris," Supreme stopped and said before going inside, "Your services will no longer be needed here." And he closed the door behind him.

Supreme didn't waste any time going upstairs. He walked with purpose on the hardwood floors to the bedroom at the end of the hallway. He had imagined killing Arnez in multiple ways, but he knew he had promised Genesis he would leave him alive if and when he found him. Supreme had every intention of keeping that promise.

The door was slightly ajar and Supreme could see Arnez sleeping. He quietly pushed the door open and walked over, sitting on the edge of the bed. He watched Arnez sleeping peacefully for a few more minutes before getting up and standing over him. Supreme pulled out his 9mm, placing it on the temple of Arnez's head, continuing to nudge it until the cold steel woke him up.

"What's going on?" Arnez mumbled not fully awake. Once Supreme used his elbow to press down on Arnez's upper chest, which was completely bandaged because of the burns he sustained, Arnez quickly woke up. "You came to kill me," he spoke with defeat in his voice.

"Slow down. One thing at a time. By the way, you look like shit."

"Where's my nurse?"

"Mrs. Harris has been let go, but she received a hefty severance pay. There's no one here to take care of you but me." Supreme smiled.

"Did you come to torture me? I told you, I didn't kill Aaliyah or Precious. I swear." Arnez's voice was weak, but his denial was strong.

"I know. Aaliyah and Precious are both alive. But you still deserve to die for taking my daughter in the first place. But we can get back to that in a minute. Unfortunately, there is nothing connecting Maya to Aaliyah's kidnapping. She's placed all the blame on you, painting herself as a victim and it's working. Currently she's facing no charges."

"That bitch Maya left me for dead. I'm stuck in this bed, barely able to walk while she walks around free, but she underestimated me. I have proof that Maya was involved."

"I was praying you would say that. I want my daughter and Precious to have peace of mind. That won't happen until Maya is either dead or locked up for the rest of her life."

"Maya thought by killing me she had tied up all the loose ends. I have to give her credit. Maya has to be my toughest opponent yet, but she underestimated me."

"How is that?"

"Maya took my cell before leaving me unconscious in a house she was trying to burn down. Luckily, I came to and I also had a backup phone she knew nothing about. If I didn't have that backup, I would be dead right now. I had that phone for insurance. I kept all our text messages, some audio and even video that proves Maya was the mastermind behind everything regarding Aaliyah's kidnapping and wanting her dead." Arnez gave a devilish laugh.

"Where's that phone? I need it."

"I'll give it to you, but can you promise me something?"

"What's that?"

"When you kill me, can you make it as painless as possible."

"Now why would I do that?"

"Because I've always been straight up with you, Supreme. Truth be told, if it wasn't for me and the money I put into your career, you probably wouldn't be the superstar you ended up being."

"How long are you going to hold that over my head?"

"For as long as you'll let me. I ain't got nothing else. I guess it don't really matter. I'm already on the brink of death."

"Where's the phone, Arnez?"

"Over there in that top drawer."

"What's the code?" Supreme asked once he retrieved the cell.

"I told you I'm always straight up with you," Arnez said after giving Supreme the code and he recovered everything he needed to make sure Maya spent the rest of her miserable life behind bars.

"You kept your word and delivered... thank you."

"I heard that if you shoot a man in the back of his head the death is so rapid you feel no pain. Can you show me your gratitude for giving you the evidence you need to bury Maya by killing me in that manner?"

"I'll do one better. I won't kill you at all."

"You're gonna let me live?" Arnez's tone was a mixture of disbelief and hope.

"Not because I want to or even think you deserve it."

"Then why?" Arnez was confused.

"Because of a promise I made to Genesis."

"Genesis? I didn't even think you were cool with Genesis."

"I'm not, but he's proven himself to be a decent man and Precious had always spoke highly of him. Genesis said you have some information that could possibly change his life, but he needs you alive to get it. So I'll be letting Genesis know your whereabouts so he can get the information he needs. Maybe if he's satisfied with what you tell him, he'll have mercy on you and let you live."

"Please. That man hates me just as much, if not more, than I hate him. I rather die at your hands than his. I'm begging you to kill me now."

"I can't do that. Some people may not like me, but most, if not all, respect me. Why... because I'm a man of my word. I promised Genesis I wouldn't kill you and that's that. What I can do is wait a couple days before letting him know where you are. For your sake, hopefully by the time he arrives you'll already be dead. Not sure how long you'll survive without Mrs. Harris here to take care of you. You're already weak. Being without food and water might be your breaking point," Supreme reasoned.

"You a cold motherfucker, Supreme."

"Nobody ever said I was the nicest guy in the world. Rest in peace, Arnez." Supreme smirked before making his exit.

"Precious, when you said you wanted to meet for lunch I didn't know what to expect. You had been ignoring my calls and every time I came to see you, Xavier told me you weren't home."

"I wasn't. If you're implying your grandson was lying, you're wrong."

"I know Xavier wouldn't lie to me. I was simply saying that you were always out of my reach."

"Let me guess. You're persistence was because you wanted to talk to me about Maya."

"Maya did tell me that you and Genesis had cornered her on a street in Harlem. She also said that you choked her and was trying to kill her. Is that true, Precious?"

"That sounds about right." Precious shrugged, drinking her water.

"You're not going to even deny you tried to kill your sister in broad daylight?"

Nope. Why would I? I'm not a liar like Maya."

"You judge your sister. But how are your actions and decisions any better than the ones you accuse Maya of?"

"Are you serious with this question," Precious scoffed.

"Very. I want to understand, but I'm having a difficult time."

"Then let me help you. I'm sure you've heard of the term psychopath before. Some of the key traits are, they feel no remorse for what they've done. When confronted with their actions, they don't show the same sort of anxiety that a non-psychopath would show. They are also extremely impulsive with their actions and are very big risk takers. But the scary part about a psychopath is that they tend to be extremely charismatic and charming individuals. Those characteristics describe Maya to a tee. The difference between Maya and me is that she is that way at all times with all people. I, on the other hand, only want to kill people that are trying to hurt my family or me. Big difference."

"We'll have to agree to disagree. Has Maya made some questionable decisions in the past, no doubt. But your sister has changed and I want this feuding between the two of you to stop. Life is too short for this bitterness you harbor for Maya."

"I'm gonna stop you right there because I'm afraid if you say another word to defend Maya, I'll change my mind about why I invited you to lunch today."

"I don't want that. The last thing this family needs is more division between us. I don't want you to shut me out too. Aaliyah still isn't taking my calls," Quentin said somberly putting his head down.

"That's actually why I wanted to see you."

"Is something wrong with Aaliyah!" Quentin sounded alarmed.

"Relax, it's nothing like that. Aaliyah and Dale got engaged."

"My granddaughter is getting married!" Precious had never seen her father smile so hard.

"Yes, she is."

"That's wonderful. I've met Dale a few times and he seems to genuinely love her."

"I get that from him too. To celebrate their engagement, I'm putting together a dinner party for family and close friends this Saturday. I would like for you to be there and so would Aaliyah."

"You mean that?" Quentin's eyes immediately watered up.

"Yes. We will never accept Maya, but Aaliyah wants to mend her relationship with you. She loves and misses you very much. We know how stubborn she can be and yes, I know she gets that from her mother." Precious giggled. "But she adores you

Quentin and so do I," she confessed. "So will you come?"

"It would take an act from God to stop me. I will be there as the proudest grandfather ever. Thank you for doing this for me, Precious." Quentin reached across the table taking his daughter's hand. "Never doubt or forget that I love you with all my heart."

"I love you too, Daddy." Precious told her father for what seemed like the very first time.

Chapter Twenty-Five

Reasons To Celebrate

As guests arrived to the restaurant on Lexington Avenue, there was no doubt that Precious spared no expense for Aaliyah's engagement party. It was a vision of contemporary luxury. The décor incorporated luxurious fabrics in a mixture of charcoal, cherry, blue, and black highlighted with silver and crystal. There were floor-to-ceiling windows with spectacular panoramic views of New York City. The central chandelier in the middle of the elaborate room changed colors to suit the mood. The walls were adorned with original paintings on silk, and lacquered enamel

and gold plated ceiling lamps fashioned to resemble birdcages.

"I'm impressed, Precious. Our daughter is going to be blown away by how beautiful this place is. I know I am," Nico stated, glancing around the restaurant.

"Thank you. I had to pay a pretty penny to reserve this place, especially at the last minute. But when the event planner showed me images of this place, I knew this was it. It is gorgeous," Precious said feeling proud of her selection.

"Almost as gorgeous as the hostess," Nico commented. He was mesmerized by how flawless Precious looked in a shimmering mesh cutout gown that fit like a glove. She wore her hair up with loose curls framing her face and a pair of reversible diamond, sapphire, and aquamarine earrings with an identical intricate diamond starburst pendant necklace set in platinum.

"Are you flirting with me, Nico?"

"Isn't a man allowed to compliment his wife?"

"You know my lawyer drafted up the annulment papers, but with everything that has been going on, I haven't had the chance to sign them. So we're married on paper only. I don't mean to be so blunt, but I don't want you to think that anything has changed."

Nico noticed Precious look over at the door when Supreme came in. "You're still hoping he'll take you back. Even when the annulment is finalized that doesn't mean Supreme will want to marry you again."

"I have a much better chance of that happening if I'm a single woman instead of a married one," Precious shot back.

"Maybe, maybe not. Regardless, I know that you love me and if you gave us a chance we would have a great marriage and grow old together."

"It wouldn't bother you that although we were married my heart belonged to Supreme?" Precious questioned.

"I know that you love me."

"I would never deny that, Nico. You're Aaliyah's father and my first love, but Supreme is my soul mate."

Nico didn't even try to hide his disgust at what Precious said.

"I know that's not what you want to hear but it's the truth. Whether Supreme takes me back or not, he will always be the love of my life." Nico uttered not a word, but shook his head. "Oh look, Aaliyah and Dale just got here." Precious was enthused and walked off in their direction.

"Mother, I can't believe how beautiful it looks in here. You did an amazing job." Aaliyah hugged her mother not wanting to let her go.

"Thank you, but I can't take all the credit. I did hire a pretty amazing event planner that brought my ideas to life. Did you see that painting I had done of you and Dale?"

"We did! How did you get that done so fast?"

"Your mother is very gifted. I have ways of making the impossible happen."

"I know you do!" Mother and daughter laughed as if sharing an inside joke.

"Mrs. Carter, thank you so much for putting together a beautiful engagement for me and Aaliyah. I'm looking forward to having you as a mother-in-law."

"Thank you, Dale. I'm looking forward to having you as a son-in-law. You make my daughter incredibly happy and that means the world to me." Precious reached over and gave Dale a hug. "Welcome to the family."

"Speaking of family, Uncle Genesis has arrived and he brought Skylar," Aaliyah said excitedly.

Precious rushed over and wrapped her arms around Skylar. "I can't believe you're here. Genesis, why didn't you tell me Skylar was home?!" Precious punched Genesis in his arm.

"I wanted it to be a surprise. I know how worried you've been and I thought this would be the perfect time to let you know it all worked out," Genesis explained.

"Thank you for your concern, Precious. I know you did everything you could to save me that day," Skylar acknowledged.

"I appreciate you saying that because the guilt was driving me crazy."

"You have nothing to feel guilty about. Arnez is the one responsible for what happened to me. No one else. But I'm home now and with the man I love.

My son and mother will be here tomorrow so I have my life back. Everything is perfect."

"Nothing will be perfect until I get my hands on Arnez. He needs to pay for what he did to you and I need for him to answer some questions for me."

"What sort of questions, Genesis?" Skylar asked.

"Nothing that would interest you."

"If you're interested then I'm interested too," Skylar said.

"We're supposed to be here celebrating Aaliyah's engagement," Precious jumped in and said. "We have more than enough time to discuss Arnez on another day. How about we go get some drinks," Precious suggested sensing that Genesis was uncomfortable with the direction the conversation was going.

"The two of you go ahead. I need to speak to Nico," Genesis told them.

While Precious and Skylar made a beeline to get some champagne, Genesis went to speak with Nico about business.

Aaliyah was preparing herself to have a pleasant conversation with Justina, who strolled in with Amir.

"I see your mother went all out," Amir said, kissing Aaliyah on the cheek.

"You know my mother. If it isn't over the top then it's not done right."

"It looks beautiful and so do you. I love what you're wearing. But you always had the best taste in clothes," Justina complimented Aaliyah on her nude

Calvin Klein two piece flowy look that showed plenty of skin."

"Thank you. You look pretty amazing yourself. I have to admit you've blossomed into a pretty gorgeous girl. Hasn't she, Amir."

"Yes, she has," Amir said looking over at Justina adoringly.

"I got you something." Justina handed Aaliyah a tiny box that contained pink diamond studded earrings. "Congratulations on your engagement."

"You didn't have to get me a gift."

"I wanted to. I also wanted to thank you for being kind enough to let me come. This is such a special day for you and for you to allow me to be a part of it truly shows what an awesome person you are."

"Honestly I wasn't sure how I was going to feel about you coming, but now that you're here, I'm glad you came." Aaliyah and Justina embraced for the first time in years. "I'm happy to have my friend back."

"I'm happy to be back."

"I guess we both should thank Amir for being so persistent." Aaliyah smiled.

"Finally, I get the credit I deserve," Amir joked.

"I hate to break up this happy reunion," Supreme came up and said. "But I need to borrow my daughter for a second. It won't take that long."

"Borrow me, Daddy. You have such a way with words," Aaliyah mocked, following her dad over to a table in the corner where they had some privacy. "What did you want to talk to me about? It must be important since you're acting so secretive." Aaliyah laughed, but Supreme didn't laugh back. "Is something wrong, Dad? You seem so serious."

"Everything will be the way it should be very soon. I found..."

"Are you all having a private father and daughter moment or are mothers welcome too," Precious said interrupting Supreme before he could finish what he was saying.

"I'm positive you'll be interested in what I'm about to tell Aaliyah so you can stay."

"Do tell, Dad! At this point I'm getting anxious."

"Yeah, please tell," Precious added.

"I got the evidence needed to make sure Maya spends the rest of her life behind bars."

"What!" both Precious and Aaliyah shouted simultaneously.

"Yes. Not only do I have proof that she was behind Aaliyah's kidnapping, but also the murder of Latreese. "

"Ohmigoodness. That means the charges against Amir will have to be dropped." Aaliyah was relieved to hear that. Even though Amir never talked about the case or Latreese, she knew having those murder charges lingering over his head was daunting.

"Supreme, you're positive Maya won't be able to squirm her way out of whatever evidence you have? That woman is a master manipulator and always manages to get away with any crime she commits," Precious said unconvinced by what Supreme had told them.

"The evidence I have is solid and bulletproof. Try as she may there is no way Maya can dispute it. She will spend the rest of her life behind bars."

"Thank you so so so so much, Daddy!" Aaliyah held onto her father for dear life. "This is the best news I've ever had."

"How did you get this evidence?" Precious was dying to know.

"The less you ladies know the better."

"Well can you at least tell us when she'll be arrested?" Precious pressed for some more info.

"First thing tomorrow morning. Something has to be resolved before that. But no worries, Maya will be off the streets for good very soon," Supreme promised.

Chapter Twenty-Six

The Ugly Truth

"Daddy! I'm so happy to see you," Maya ran up to Quentin and said when he came through the front door. "I've been going crazy being in the house by myself. I know you wanted to keep me safe, but I was feeling like a prisoner.

"Under the circumstances I didn't have much of a choice."

"I know. If it wasn't for that crazy Precious trying her best to not only ruin my life, but also kill me, none of this would be happening to me. It's horrible that she would put you in the middle of this, Daddy.

She's so selfish. Were you able to convince her to leave me the hell alone or is she still adamant that I'm the enemy?" Maya had her arms crossed and was tapping the floor with her foot growing impatient.

"I did meet with Precious for lunch. She invited me to Aaliyah's engagement party."

"Aaliyah is getting married! Humph, who would want to marry that spoiled brat? Surely not Amir... oh, let me guess, Dale. When is the party?"

"Tonight. I'm headed over there after I leave here."

"That's why you look so handsome in your suit and tie. I'm happy for you, Daddy. I'm not a fan of Aaliyah, but I know how much you love her."

"Yes, I do. I love my granddaughter very much. I love you very much too, Maya."

"I know that. If you think I'm going to feel like you're a traitor for going to Aaliyah's engagement party, you don't have to be concerned. I understand that Aaliyah and Precious are your family too, even though they continue to do everything in their power to turn you against me. But you see through their lies and know the truth. Thank you for always being in my corner, Daddy." Maya hugged Quentin and he held her tightly, rubbing her back lovingly.

"I know I'm responsible for a lot of your issues and I'll go to my grave never forgiving myself," Quentin whispered in Maya's ears.

"Daddy stop it! Those issues are ancient history. We've worked past that. I'm a changed woman because of you. If only Precious and the rest of her crew would realize that and let me be great. Gosh, I'm so sick of their holier than though attitude when all of them are nothing but a bunch of criminals their damn selves."

"Maya, I know the truth."

"Of course you know the truth. Duh! That's why you're trying to get Precious to call off her goons and let me live my life in peace. Hell, doesn't she have a divorce or a marriage to figure out. But hey, I can't keep up when it comes to my dear sister," Maya huffed.

"I know the truth about you."

"I'm not following you, Daddy," Maya said coyly, putting her hair behind her ear.

"I was always your biggest advocate... blindly so. No matter what Precious, Aaliyah, or anyone else would say, I believed you."

"As you should, Daddy. You know my heart and what a good person I am. You also know how much I love you and I would never, ever do anything to disappoint you."

"So why would you kidnap my granddaughter. Why? Why would you work with Arnez and orchestrate the take down of my family and our business? I've done nothing but love you, but all this time you've been out to destroy the people I love."

"They've finally gotten to you. You believe all those nasty lies that they're spreading about me. How could you believe them? You know me, Daddy. I could never do the things that Precious and Aaliyah have accused me of. They've contaminated your mind with their malicious lies. You can't let them win," Maya pleaded.

"No, it's you! You, Maya, that has forced malicious lies on me. It wasn't Precious or Aaliyah that opened my eyes to the person you are. Supreme came to me and showed me the proof. Supreme! He wanted me to see for myself that I was supporting the wrong daughter. Where did I go wrong with you? Was your childhood so damaged that there is no fixing you?" Quentin could no longer keep his composure and broke down crying. "I truly believed my love would cure whatever demons you were fighting, but I've lost that war."

"What sort of proof does Supreme have?" Maya questioned, having no concern for how emotionally broken her father was, but worried about protecting her own ass.

"He has the sort of proof that makes you lucky the state of New York no longer imposes the death penalty."

Maya swallowed hard realizing the walls have finally closed in on her, but she wasn't willing to give up so easily. "They don't give the death penalty for kidnapping."

"True, but premeditated murder with special circumstances will have you spending the rest of your life behind bars."

"I didn't murder anyone," Maya lied.

"You're still in denial." He shook his head.

"Yes, I'll admit I helped Arnez kidnap Aaliyah, but he left me no choice. He threatened to kill me if I didn't do what he said. I wanted to tell you the truth, but I was afraid for my life. I thought he would come back and kill me. He said he would kill you too. I was only trying to protect us, father. You have to believe me!" she begged.

"If you would've spun this story yesterday, I would have, but I know the truth now. You are the one who killed Latreese and set up Amir to take the fall. You left Arnez for dead after you burned down the house he was staying at."

As Quentin continued to name the shenanigans that Maya had spearheaded she shut him out and was no longer listening. Once he mentioned her murdering Latreese, Maya knew it was over for her. There was no coming back from that. The best attorney in the country wouldn't be able to beat those charges. Latreese's death was brutal and any jury would want to make sure she paid the ultimate price.

"Maya, you're going to spend the rest of your life behind bars and even if I wanted to, there is nothing I can do to help you this time. But I've finally accepted that although you're my daughter and I love you with all my heart, being locked up is exactly where you need to be."

"I'm surprised Quentin isn't here yet," Precious commented to Supreme after glancing down at her watch. "He was thrilled about me inviting him to Aaliyah's engagement party. He wouldn't miss it for anything.

"I'm sure he'll be here soon. He's probably making his peace with Maya before he comes."

"His peace with Maya. Quentin knows?"

"Yes. That was what I was referring to when I said something had to be resolved. Quentin was the first person I showed the evidence to. I thought he needed to know instead of finding out on the news after Maya was arrested."

"That was very considerate of you, Supreme. I'm sure Quentin was grateful."

"Yes, he was. He's a good man. Unfortunately his love for Maya blinded him to the ugly truth. He was crushed when I showed him the evidence. He had to sit down. I thought that man was literally about to have a heartattack. She did a number on that man mentally. He wasn't ready to face the fact that his daughter was a monster."

"I can believe that. When I saw him the other day he was still defending and protecting Maya. As much as I loathe her, it makes me sad what this is going to do to Quentin, but he needed to know the truth," Precious reasoned.

"He did and by the time I left he realized that too. All he asked was that I give him time to confront Maya and get closure before I turned everything over to the police. I gave him until tomorrow morning."

"I know Maya is going to come up with every excuse in the world to try and make herself out to be the victim. Once she sees that Quentin is not falling for her bullshit, Maya is gonna go crazy. I wish I could be a fly on the wall to see her have one of her monumental temper tantrums." Precious giggled.

Maya stood over Quentin scrutinizing his motionless, dead body. It all happened so fast that her father's mouth was still wide open from the shock of his daughter firing three bullets in his chest. When Maya casually picked up her purse, Quentin had no idea it was because she wanted to retrieve her gun. Unbeknownst to him, she didn't leave the house without it.

Quentin made the fatal mistake of believing that once confronted with the truth, Maya would throw in the towel and take her impending jail stay like a trooper. That mistake cost him his life. His warm blood was streaming across the marble floor. He was dressed for a celebration, but instead Quentin's attire was more casket ready.

"Damn you, Precious! All your whining got Supreme involved and there he went playing hero. I'm sure you're somewhere gloating thinking you're still the Queen B. Your superior attitude cost our father his life. He's dead because of you. Sorry, Daddy." Maya bent down over his dead body and stroked his hair. "I didn't want to kill you, but you left me no choice. We both know I'm not cut out for jail. The color orange doesn't even look good on me. I've got to get out of town. Luckily, I have plenty of money to live a wonderful life on the run. But before I go, I have some unfinished business to attend to. I'll definitely be leaving New York with a bang."

Maya took her fingers and closed her father's open eyes before kissing him goodbye on the lips.

Chapter Twenty-Seven

Death Becomes Her

"This has been the most amazing night," Aaliyah said as she slow danced with Dale.

"It really has been. Your mother did an incredible job. You're lucky to have her."

"Yes, I am. We've been through so much together. Sometimes I almost forget she's my mom because she's also my best friend. But she's quick to remind me that she's mama bear and I'm baby bear." Aaliyah laughed.

"I understand where you're coming from. Emory was more than my brother, he was also my best friend. He used some questionable tactics, but he always had my back. He should be here with me right now celebrating our engagement and be my best man at our wedding."

"I know you miss your brother. It hurts me to my heart seeing that pain in your eyes. I'm afraid it won't ever go away."

"Yes, it will as soon as I get justice for my brother. That will come in the form of retribution to the motherfucker that killed him."

Aaliyah placed her head on Dale's chest relishing how content she felt in his arms. But as content as she was, there was no shaking her fear. The fear that one day her secret would be revealed. Dale would learn that the person he's determined to seek retribution on is her father.

"Aaliyah and Dale look so happy dancing right now. It reminds me of when we danced at our wedding reception," Precious said to Supreme.

"They do seem happy. Hopefully it will last."

"Why wouldn't it?" Precious was taken aback by Supreme's comment.

"They're both young."

"And? They're older than we were when we got married."

"True, but look at us. Our marriage didn't last," Supreme pointed out.

"Okay, but we had a lot of great years and we're parents to two beautiful kids. I have no regrets." Precious's tone had become defensive. "Do you regret us getting married?"

"Of course not. With all the hell we've been through together, there has never been a moment that I've regretted making you my wife."

"I could be your wife again." Precious leaned in and kissed Supreme, wanting to seize an opportunity. He reciprocated and they were tonguing each other down like a couple of teenagers at a drive-in movie.

"I don't think this is the time or place for us to be doing this," Supreme said pulling away from Precious.

"You might be right, but my condo isn't too far from here. Everyone is having a great time. No one will even notice if we sneak out of here."

"I don't think that's a good idea."

"You need to stop fighting the inevitable. We belong together, Supreme."

"I'm not the one that's married."

"On paper only. Nico knows that my attorney has already drawn up the annulment papers. All I have to do is sign them and I'll be a free woman. Free to marry the man I'm in love with which is you. You and I both know we're meant to spend the rest of our lives together. Now let's go home." Precious glanced up giving her best bedroom eyes.

"You're too much." Supreme grinned.

"Before you decide just think about what I said. Don't answer yet. Quentin just texted me saying he's out front and wants me to come outside."

"Why doesn't he just come in?"

"I'm sure he's burden with guilt about Maya. Quentin probably doesn't feel comfortable facing Aaliyah after taking Maya's side for so long. I'm gonna go out there and talk to him. He needs to know that we forgive him and he doesn't have to feel ashamed to show his face because we're family."

"That's very mature and daughter-like of you, Precious."

"Thank you. I'm simply following your lead. So stay right here, I'll be right back." Precious winked her eye and blew a kiss at Supreme, which he caught and blew one in return. "I'm getting my man back," Precious said under her breath while heading out to meet Quentin.

"I wonder where my mom is going," Aaliyah pondered out loud while talking to Justina and Amir.

"Who knows. Maybe she's stepping out to get some fresh air," Justina said. "Speaking of stepping out. Amir, can I have your car keys. I left my cell in your car and I need to get it. My boyfriend might be trying to call me."

"You have a boyfriend?" Aaliyah and Amir both blurted out.

"Yes. Why do you guys sound so surprised. "

"It's just that you never mentioned having a man." Amir couldn't hide his displeasure.

"He doesn't live here. It's a long distance relationship, but we're trying to make it work. That's why I need to get my phone because if he calls and he can't get ahold of me, he'll think I'm with another man. He's the jealous type."

"Well, technically you are out with another man." Aaliyah smiled.

"Amir doesn't count. We're more like besties than anything else. So let me get those keys."

Amir handed his keys to Justina and was feeling some kinda way that Justina had a man. He was secretly hoping that maybe they could give their relationship a try again now that they were older and more mature.

"I'll walk out with you, Justina. I wanna chat with my mom anyway. We'll be back, Amir." Aaliyah waved and made a silly face at Amir when Justina wasn't looking. She could tell his feelings were hurt over what Justina said. She thought it was kinda cute. Now that Aaliyah had fallen in love and was getting married she wanted Amir to be happy too. Especially after the horrific way Latreese was killed and then he was charged with her murder. Aaliyah felt that Justina seemed to be in a much better place now and could possibly be a good match for Amir. Besides her, who knew him better than Justina since they were all childhood friends.

"I'll be right back. Amir parked across the street," Justina told Aaliyah.

"Okay. I'ma look for my mom. If I'm not here when you come back, I'll see you inside," Aaliyah said, heading down the block.

"Sure thing." When Justina opened the passenger door of the Range Rover she was expecting to see her phone in the console or on the seat, but it wasn't there. She then looked under the seat thinking that maybe it fell. "Where the hell is my phone!" she yelled bending over. At first Justina didn't see her phone, but she did notice a handgun. "You really need to remember to put your toys away, Amir." She laughed before noticing her cell nestled between the floor on the side of the car seat. "There you go!"

Justina closed and locked the door before heading back across the street. She was about to go inside until she heard what sounded like muffled screams. Justina walked with caution down the dark block to see what was going on. As she got closer, there was some sort of scuffle going on. It was obviously Aaliyah, but she couldn't see who she was fighting with. Justina took her heels off so she could tip-toe even closer without being heard, but she was able to hear plenty.

"Yo' ass always interrupting some shit!" Maya screamed at Aaliyah as she tried to keep her hand pressed over Aaliyah's mouth so no one could hear what was going on. But Aaliyah was doing her best to fight back, but it was difficult since Maya had a gun in the other hand. "Don't make me shoot you right here," Maya threatened.

Aaliyah refused to give up though. She bit down on Maya's hand as hard as she could. "You bitch!" Maya wailed in pain releasing her hand from over Aaliyah's mouth. Aaliyah used the opportunity to turn around and kick Maya in the stomach. Maya flew back, falling on the sidewalk and dropping her gun. She quickly regained her composure as both women lunged towards the weapon.

"You will die tonight, Maya!" Aaliyah barked as the women struggled for the gun.

"Not if I kill you first," Maya shot back. But she was about to eat those words when Aaliyah got the upper hand by grabbing ahold of the gun. Not one to be easily defeated, Maya noticed a large rock. Without giving it a second thought, she grabbed the rock, pouncing it on the side of Aaliyah's head.

"Oh fuck," Aaliyah mumbled, grabbing her now bleeding head and falling over to the ground. The hit didn't knock her out cold, but it did leave her disoriented. Maya then returned the favor and snatched the gun pointing it directly at Aaliyah's head.

"You shoulda stayed yo' ass inside your lil' engagement party instead of coming out here looking for mother," Maya said shaking her head.

"I was gonna drag yo' worrisome ass wit' me but hell no! I'ma kill you right now 'cause you ain't nothing but trouble," Maya spit cocking her gun.

"If you kill me, Maya, no one in my family will rest until they hunt you down and kill you."

"Whatever! You're just more dead weight added to my already mounting body count. The only difference is I'm going to take great pleasure in watching the life leave your pathetic body. Bye Bye, Aaliyah."

Aaliyah closed her eyes and folded her hands, resigned to her fate of death. When the sound of the gunshots ricocheted through the air, Aaliyah's only prayer was to be with her mother in heaven. A few seconds went by and Aaliyah was waiting for some sort of excruciating pain to explode through her body, but she felt nothing. She then thought that maybe her fear of dying had made her completely numb. But after a few more seconds of feeling nothing she opened her eyes and saw Justina holding a gun and Maya was spread out on the sidewalk. She was lying in a pool of blood.

"Aaliyah, are you okay?!" Justina rushed over to her to make sure she wasn't hurt.

"I'm alive," she stuttered in shock. "What about my mother? I think she's dead. Maya killed her. Give me your gun," she said snatching it from Justina. "I wanna make sure Maya can't get away." Aaliyah jumped up.

"Maya isn't going anywhere, Aaliyah. I already checked her pulse. She's dead."

Not wanting to celebrate prematurely, Aaliyah had to check herself to make sure Maya was really dead. She checked for a pulse, heartbeat, and made sure she wasn't breathing. "Burning in hell for eternity is even too good for you," Aaliyah glared at Maya's lifeless body and said.

Aaliyah then rushed over to the car where her mother was. Precious's body was slumped over in the backseat. "Justina, go get both my dads. Let them know that my mother is dead. I don't wanna leave her," Aaliyah cried.

Justina rushed inside to the restaurant while Aaliyah stayed in the backseat of the car, holding her mother crying frantically. "Why... why did you have to take my mother," Aaliyah kept saying repeatedly.

"Aaliyah, what's wrong? Why are you crying, baby," Precious slurred in a low tone.

"Mommy, you're alive. Maya said she killed you. I can't believe you're alive." Aaliyah began crying even harder, but this time it was tears of joy.

"Oohhhh," Precious mumbled. "I should've known it was Maya that hit me in the back of the head. I must've been knocked unconscious. Damn, my head is throbbing, but I'm alive so it's all good." Precious gave a slight smile.

"Yes, you're alive and Maya is dead. All is finally right in the world."

Chapter Twenty-Eight

Lost One

"I can't get over how crazy last night turned out to be," Skylar said taking the dishes from the table after her and Genesis finished eating breakfast.

"I know. We were supposed to be celebrating Aaliyah's engagement and instead she almost died and so did Precious. We all knew that Maya was dangerous, but she had become completely unhinged."

"Well on the bright side, Maya's reign of terror is officially over. Now that she's dead, she can't hurt anybody ever again."

"True, but now that Maya's dead, I might not ever know the truth."

"The truth about what?' Skylar asked confused.

"Don't worry about it. It doesn't concern you."

"Genesis, we're in a committed relationship. Whatever concerns you concerns me too."

Genesis wavered before continuing. "It's about my wife, Talisa."

"What about her?"

"She might be alive."

Skylar almost dropped the plates when Genesis spoke those words. "Why would you think that?" Skylar stayed calm, but her worst fear was beginning to surface.

"Because after Arnez had you kidnapped he called me. He said that Talisa was alive. That's why I asked you was there anyone else on the island with you. The way Arnez's sick mind thinks, he wouldn't be able to resist such a diabolical twist. Are you sure nobody else was there? Maybe they kept the two of you separated and you didn't see her."

"I guess that could be possible, but it seems highly unlikely. I was there for a while and the island wasn't that big. I'm sure I would've seen her if she was on the island."

"I guess I was wrong." Genesis got up from the table frustrated. "Maybe Arnez has Talisa hidden somewhere else," he considered.

"Or maybe Arnez was lying to you and Talisa is dead."

"Maybe, but that's not Arnez's MO. Damn! Maya was evil and she had to go, but I wish she didn't have to go just yet. She was my last hope to find Talisa. The truth probably died with her." Genesis sighed.

"You're still in love with her aren't you?"

"Of course I love her. I'll always love Talisa and if she's out there, I want to find her and bring her home."

"She's dead and I'm alive. Isn't that enough for you, Genesis. We're supposed to be a family. How can we make that happen if you're fixated on your dead wife?"

"I'm not fixated. I want the truth. Never for a second did I believe there was any chance Talisa was alive. But now I can't shake believing that she is."

Skylar was crying her heart out on the inside. Genesis didn't have to say it, but it was obvious to her that if Talisa walked through those doors right now she would be history. Skylar believed that her and Genesis shared the sort of love that would trump anything including his supposed to be dead wife. Leaving Talisa on the island was to guarantee that the past wouldn't haunt the present or their future together. Unfortunately, Skylar didn't count on Arnez dangling the truth in Genesis's face.

"I don't want to live like this. I genuinely believed that you loved me and wanted to spend your life with me."

"Skylar, I do love you. You and your son have brought so much happiness into my life. You have to believe that."

"I do believe you, but I want you to answer a question for me and I want the truth, Genesis."

"Ask the question."

"If Arnez was telling you the truth and Talisa was still alive, what would that mean for us?"

"I would make sure that you and your son are well provided for, but Talisa is my wife. My life would be with her."

Skylar immediately broke down and began crying.

"Skylar you asked me for the truth."

"I know that, but I guess hearing the truth cut deeper then I thought it would."

"It doesn't matter anyway. I think you and everyone else is right. Arnez was simply playing a sick joke on me. Talisa isn't alive. She's dead."

Skylar was now flooded with guilt. Talisa was very much alive and stuck on the island she escaped from. "Genesis, I have something to tell you," Skylar said, wiping away her tears."

"What is it?" Before Skyler could respond there was a knock at the door. "One second, Skylar. I need to get the door. It might be Nico with some information about Quentin. Nobody can seem to get ahold of him. We want to tell him about Maya before he hears it on the news or radio."

"No problem. I'ma go freshen up," she said still wiping away her tears. Skylar was thankful they were interrupted by the knock at the door because she was about to come clean with Genesis and once

she did there was no turning back. Once he learned that she lied to him about Talisa, he would probably hate her so Skylar was in no rush to reveal the truth. But she made up her mind that it had to be done today before she lost her nerves.

The knocking at the door grew louder as Genesis hurried to open it. "Hold on, Nico," he huffed out loud as the knocking had now turned into banging. But when Genesis opened the door he was in for a rude awakening.

"Genesis Taylor, turn around and put your hands behind your back. You're under arrest for operating a continuing criminal enterprise. You're looking at a pine box sentence," one of the DEA agents joked while handcuffing him.

Genesis didn't let the taunt shake him. He remained calm, complying to what he was told and not allowing himself to become overwhelmed by the dozens of DEA agents at his front door. Skylar on the other hand wasn't as composed.

"Omigosh! Genesis, why are you under arrest. Where are you taking him?!" Skylar continued to ramble as her entire body was shaking hysterically.

"Your boyfriend here will be spending the rest of his life in a Federal Prison. If you don't sit down and have a seat, you'll be joining him," the agent threatened.

"Skylar, call my attorney." That's all Genesis said as he was escorted out of his penthouse in handcuffs. Then his mind shifted to the new connect and how the shipment he was supposed to receive never came. "I done fucked up," Genesis mumbled under his breath on the ride down the elevator to the awaiting vehicle that would be transporting him to a federal prison.

"Aaliyah, I'm glad you're here too," Nico said kissing her on the cheek when she let him into Precious's condo. "How are both of you feeling?"

"Excellent. Nothing some extra strength Excedrin couldn't cure. Right, Mom?" Aaliyah smiled at her mother.

"That would be correct. Mother and daughter are being well taken care of. Xavier actually went out to pick up our favorite Chinese food and some wine."

"Yes, some wine! Just what we need to celebrate no longer having Maya around to make our lives miserable. Life is good!"

"Before the two of you celebrate, Maya made sure to leave us with even more misery," Nico stated gravely.

"What are you talking about, Daddy?"

"Yeah, Nico. Maya wasn't expecting to die last night. She didn't have enough time to do anything horrible enough to bring all of us misery," Precious scoffed.

"Not true. There's no easy way to tell both of

you this but..." Nico started to get choked up.

"Daddy, what is it! You're scaring me."

"Yes, Nico! Would you spit it out?!" The anticipation of waiting to hear what Nico had to say made Precious ready to throw a vase at his head.

"It's Quentin," Nico muttered.

"Oh gosh! Hearing about Maya's death probably gave him a heart attack," Aaliyah said covering her mouth in distress. "What hospital is he at? Come on, Mom, we have to go see him."

"Let me get my stuff," Precious said standing up.

"Wait! Both of you, just wait. Quentin isn't at the hospital, he's at the morgue."

"No... no, no, no, no, no!" Precious wept.

"Not my Grandfather!" Aaliyah hollered and fell to the floor. Precious went over to Aaliyah and held her, as mother and daughter mourned for Quentin together.

Chapter Twenty-Nine

Brand New Me

"Damn, Justina, you feel so good," Markell moaned with each stroke. He wanted to fuck and make love to her at the same time. He gently kissed her lips, neck, traveling down to her breasts, putting her nipples in his mouth. But each thrust became more powerful as he wanted to go deeper inside Justina's dripping wet pussy.

"Harder!" Justina purred in Markell's ear making his dick even harder. He kept going until he eventually collapsed in her arms.

"I love you," Markell said in Justina's ear after

they both climaxed.

"I love you, too."

Markell rolled his body from on top of Justina and stared up at the ceiling fan before lighting up a cigarette. "Is it possible that sex keeps getting better with you? I can't get enough. I wanna lay inside of you forever," he said.

Justina gave a slight laugh. "I'm glad you find me so irresistible," she teased, nibbling his neck.

"I do. Too irresistible, so much so that I can't leave you alone."

"Who said you had to?"

"I can only imagine the look on T-Roc's face when he finds out I'm bangin' his daughter."

"Shut up!" Justina playfully hit Markell over the face with the pillow.

"Chill. You don't wanna make nothing catch on fire," he said taking another pull from his cigarette. "But on the real, I think it's time we make it known that we're a couple."

"Not yet. Let's wait until things cool down a little more. I mean the police just stopped questioning me about killing Maya. I still can't believe how well that worked out. I knew eventually I would have to kill her, but saving Aaliyah's life in the process was a major bonus," Justina beamed.

"Word. I have to admit we played that nicely. I worked Arnez and you worked Maya. We were able to get rid of both of them and keep our hands clean in the process."

"I still remember when Maya approached me about helping her get revenge on Precious and the rest of the clan. She thought I was a dumb, naïve, silly girl. The perfect person to be her personal puppet in the game she was playing. Little did Maya know I was in control and she was playing my game."

"So what's next?"

"Aaliyah trusts me now. She wants to be besties again especially now that I saved her life. But I'll never forget how she and Amir betrayed me. She thinks now that she's done with Amir, she can run off and get married and live happily ever after." Justina began to laugh hysterically. "But that's never gonna happen. Once Dale finds out that Supreme is the one that killed his brother, he'll dump Aaliyah's ass so fast. He might even be so pissed at her for keeping the truth from him, he'll kill Aaliyah himself and save me the trouble. But honestly, I have no interest in killing Aaliyah. If I really wanted her dead, I would've came back and finished the job after I attacked her at the hospital. It's way too easy to just let her die though. I"ll have much more fun watching her suffer."

"Baby, you don't need to worry about Aaliyah or Amir anymore. They've both suffered enough. Amir's dad is facing life in Federal Prison and Aaliyah and her family has lost Quentin. We have more money then we can spend and we're in love. We can leave today and retire on some exotic island. Just the two of us."

"I knew you would say that."

"Of course I would say that. I'm in love with you. I feel like the luckiest man in the world." Markell leaned over and kissed Justina passionately.

She returned the kiss and whispered, "Taste it, baby."

"I can't get enough of you," Markell said putting his tongue between her legs and slowly licking her clit.

Unfortunately for Markell, no matter how exceptional his fuck and tongue game was, he was no longer an asset to Justina just a liability. She had other plans and none of them included Markell. She reached under the pillow, retrieving the gun she had placed there earlier when he had stepped out the room.

Markell's head was completely buried in Justina's sugar walls that when she pointed the tip of the gun at his head, he was oblivious to what was about to happen next. By the time Justina pulled the trigger and released the bullet, Markell was already a dead man.

"I was surprised when I saw your name on my visitation list," Genesis stated to Supreme when he arrived to see him.

"I wanted to come sooner, but my attorney had

to do some maneuvering to get me here. They're keeping a close eye on you. It's not surprising. This is a major case for the DEA."

"Don't remind me," Genesis grumbled putting his head down for a second. "No disrespect, Supreme, but we aren't exactly close. Why did you go out your way to come see me?"

"Our kids grew up together and you've always been there for Precious. Let's say I want to return the favor."

"Unless you can miraculously make these charges go away, I'm not sure what sort of favor you can do for me."

"I can't do that, but I do believe you can beat the case. John Gotti was able to do it, so can you. Having the best criminal attorney in New York City helps too. And hopefully what I'm about to tell you next will give you the motivation to not only fight the case, but do whatever necessary to win."

"What in the world can you tell me that will make me see a ray of light within this cage."

"I'm not going to get into details about how I obtained the information. All I'll say is, I got it from the same source that I got the Maya evidence."

"What information?"

"You're wife is alive."

Genesis's bottom lip began to quiver. It took every once of strength in his body not to break down in the visitation room in front of everyone and cry like a baby. But he was well aware this wasn't the

place to show any weakness.

"I know this is overwhelming, especially hearing it while you locked up, 'cause you feel helpless. But if you give me the okay, I'll have my men locate your wife and bring her home to you."

"You would do that for me, but why?"

"You've always been a decent man, Genesis. You've shown my daughter nothing but love and Precious, although we're no longer married, she's still my family. Arnez did the unthinkable keeping your wife from you and I want to make it right."

"I owe you, man. I mean sincerely. I promise I will repay you for this."

"You wanna know how you can repay me."

"Tell me because I'll do whatever it is."

"Beat this motherfuckin' case."

Supreme and Genesis nodded their heads in a display of unanimity.

Two Months Later...

The Final Chapter

"This is the third day in a row I've woken up in your arms. Don't you think it's time for you to move in?" Precious asked Supreme while they lay in bed. "Especially now that Xavier has gone off to college. I could use the company."

"Oh, you wanna use me for company 'cause you lonely. Nah, I'll pass."

"Supreme!" Precious rose up to stare him in the face. "Stop trying to find excuses to not make this happen. I'm no longer a married woman. I'm also a changed woman."

"Changed how?" Supreme questioned, needing Precious to explain herself. "I haven't noticed a change in you."

"They're more subtle changes that will take time for you to notice. That's why you need to move in so you can get a firsthand view."

"Oh, really."

"Yes, really."

"Let's say that we did decide to move in with each other. Your place is a tad bit too small for me. But I still have the estate in New Jersey where there is more than enough room to accommodate both of us," Supreme suggested.

"I guess I would be willing to compromise. We can always keep my condo for times we want to chill in the city."

"That sounds doable," Supreme agreed.

"Does that mean you're ready and willing to give us another try?"

"Are you willing to not drive me crazy?" Supreme asked.

"Hmmm... I can't promise you anything, but I will make a genuine go at it. So what do you say Xavier Mills. Are we about to begin a new chapter in our not so storybook yet incredibly romantic love life?"

"I wouldn't want it any other way. Love for life... remember."

"How could I forget." Precious smiled as she and Supreme made love like it was the very first time.

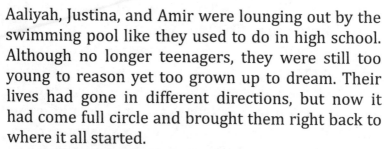

Aaliyah, Justina, and Amir were lounging out by the swimming pool like they used to do in high school. Although no longer teenagers, they were still too young to reason yet too grown up to dream. Their lives had gone in different directions, but now it had come full circle and brought them right back to where it all started.

"Justina, I know I've said it before, but I have to say it again. Thank you for saving my life. I'll never be able to tell you enough how grateful I am. You saved my mother's life too. Because after Maya killed me, trust my mother was next."

"No doubt." Amir nodded. "Maya had all her shit planned out. Thank goodness you were there, Justina, or the three of us wouldn't be sitting here right now."

"Amir's right. My grandfather's funeral wouldn't have been the only one you all attended. It would've been mine and my mother's too."

"Luckily for all of us that isn't the case," Justina said. "I've never killed anyone before and I hope I'll never have to do so again. But I'm glad I was there to save your life. I feel like now we're closer than ever."

"Yes, we are." Aaliyah reached over and hugged Justina. "I'm so happy you're going to be the maid of honor in my wedding."

"I feel so honored that you asked me to be."

"No one else deserves it more than you. I still can't believe in a few short months, I'll be a married woman," Aaliyah said excitedly. "Now all I have to do is figure out a way to convince Nico and Supreme that I want both of them to walk me down the aisle." The three of them couldn't help but laugh.

"Are you inviting your boyfriend, Justina? I would love to meet him."

"We broke up."

"Why... what happened?'

"The long distance between us was just too much. He was finding it difficult to trust me. The constant questioning was becoming overwhelming.

"I'm so sorry, Justina."

"Don't be," Amir was quick to say touching Justina's leg. "I've been helping her through the breakup, so she's doing just fine." Amir and Justina exchanged flirty stares.

"Does that mean the two of you are dating?" Aaliyah gasped.

"That's exactly what it means," Amir was more than happy to reveal.

"I'm so happy for the two of you. We all have like the best life ever," Aaliyah beamed looking down at her cell phone. "Oh I better get this, it's my mother. Hey, Mom. What's up?"

"Aaliyah, it's your father. I just got a call that he's been shot."

"Supreme?"

"No, Nico. He was shot in Miami. I'm taking the

next flight out."

"I'm coming with you."

"Okay. I'll pick you up on my way to the airport."

"Aaliyah, what happened?" Justina asked after she got off the phone.

"It's Nico. He's been shot," Aaliyah cried. "I have to get ready. My mom is gonna pick me up so we can go to Miami."

"I'll come with you. You need all the support you can get."

"You would do that for me, Justina?"

"Of course. You're my best friend," Justina avowed. Unbeknownst to Aaliyah, Justina was far from a best friend instead she was her most deadly enemy yet.

Can Genesis beat his drug charges and reunite with his wife Talisa…. Find out in

Stackin' Paper Part 3

Will Nico survive being shot and will Aaliyah make it down the aisle… Find out in

Female Hustler Part 3

All I See Is The Money...

Female 3
Hustler

A Novel

JOY DEJA KING

Keep The Family Close...

Raised By Wolves

Chapter One

"Alejo, we've been doing business for many years and my intention is for there to be many more. But I do have some concerns..."

"That's why we're meeting today," Alejo interjected, cutting Allen off. I've made you a very wealthy man. You've made millions and millions of dollars from my family..."

"And you've made that and much more from our family," Clayton snapped, this time being the one to cut Alejo off. "So lets acknowledge this being a mutual beneficial relationship between both of our families."

Alejo cut his eyes at Clayton, feeling disrespected his anger rested upon him. Clayton was the youngest son of Allen Collins but also the most vocal. Alejo then turned towards his eldest son Damacio who sat calmly not saying a word in his father's defense, which further enraged the dictator of the Hernandez family.

An ominous quietness engulfed the room as the Collins family remained seated on one side of the table and the Hernandez family occupied the other.

"I think we can agree that over the years we've created a successful business relationship that works for all parties involved," Kasir spoke up and said, trying to be the voice of reason and peacemaker for what was quickly turning into enemy territory. "No one wants to create new problems. We only want to fix the one we currently have so we can all move forward."

"Kasir, I've always liked you," Alejo said with a half smile. "You've continuously conducted yourself with class and respect. Others can learn a lot from you."

"Others, meaning your crooked ass nephews," Clayton barked not ignoring the jab Alejo was taking at him. He then pointed his finger at Felipe and Hector, making sure that everyone at the table knew exactly who he was speaking of since there was a dozen family members on the Hernandez side of the table.

Chaos quickly erupted within the Hernandez family as the members began having a heated exchange amongst each other. They were speaking Spanish and although Allen nor Clayton understood what was being said, Kasir spoke the language fluently.

"Dad, I think we need to fall back and not let this meeting get any further out of control. Lets table this discussion for a later date," Kasir told his father in a very low tone.

"Fuck that! We ain't tabling shit. As much money as we bring to this fuckin' table and these snakes want to short us. Nah, I ain't having it. That shit ends today," Clayton stated, not backing down.

"You come here and insult me and my family with your outrageous accusations," Alejo stood up and yelled, pushing back the single silver curl that kept falling over his forehead. I will not tolerate such insults from the likes of you. My family does good business. You clearly cannot say the same."

"This is what you call good business," Clayton shot back, placing his iPhone on the center of the table. Then pressing play on the video that was sent to him.

Alejo grabbed the phone from off the table and watched the video intently, scrutinizing every detail. After he was satisfied he then handed it to his son Damacio, who after viewing, passed it around to the other family members at the table.

"What's on that video?" Kasir questioned his brother.

"I want to know the same thing," his father stated.

"Lets just say that not only is those two motherfuckers stealing from us, they stealing from they own fuckin' family too," Clayton huffed, leaning back in his chair, pleased that he had the proof to back up his claims.

"We owe your family an apology," Damacio said, as his father sat back down in his chair with a glaze of defeat in his eyes. It was obvious the old man hated to be wrong and had no intentions of admitting it, so his son had to do it for him.

"Does that mean my concerns will be addressed and handled properly?" Allen Collins questioned.

"Of course. You have my word that this matter will be corrected in the very near future and there is no need for you to worry, as it won't happen again. Please accept my apology on behalf of my entire family," Damacio said, reaching over to shake each of their hand.

"Thank you, Damacio," Allen said giving a firm handshake. "I'll be in touch soon."

"Of course. Business will resume as usual and we look forward to it," Damacio made clear before the men gathered their belongings and began to make their exit.

"Wait!" the Collins men stopped in their tracks and turned towards Alejo who had shouted for them to wait.

"Father, what are you doing?" Damacio asked, confused by his father's sudden outburst.

"There is something that needs to be addressed and no one is leaving this room until it's done," Alejo demanded.

With smooth ease, Clayton rested his arm towards the back of his pants, placing his hand on the Glock 20-10mm auto. Before the meeting, the Collins' men had agreed to have their security team wait outside in the parking lot instead of coming in the building, so it wouldn't be a hostile environment. But that didn't stop Clayton from taking his own precautions. He eyed his brother Kasir who maintained his typical calm demeanor that annoyed the fuck out of Clayton.

"Alejo, what else needs to be said that wasn't already discussed?" Allen asked, showing no signs of distress.

"Please, come take a seat," Alejo said politely. Allen stared at Alejo then turned to his two sons and nodded his head as the three men walk back towards their chairs.

Alejo wasted no time and immediately began his over the top speech. "I was born in Mexico and raised by wolves. I was taught that you kill or be killed. When I rose to power by slaughtering my enemies and my friends, I felt no shame." Alejo stated looking around at everyone sitting at the table. His son Damacio swallowed hard as his adam's apple seemed to be throbbing out of his neck.

"As I got older and had my own family, I decided I didn't want that for my children. I wanted them to understand the importance of loyalty, honor and respect," Alejo said proudly, speaking with his thick Spanish accent, which was heavier than usual. He moved away from his chair and began to pace the floor as his spoke. "Without understanding the meaning of being loyal, honoring and respecting your family, you're worthless. Family forgives but some things are unforgivable so you have no place on this earth or in my family."

Then without warning and before anyone had even noticed, all you saw was blood squirting from Felipe's slit throat. Then with the same precision and quickness, Alejo took his sharp pocketknife and slit Hector's throat too. Everyone was too stunned and taken aback to stutter a word.

Alejo then wiped the blood off his pocketknife on the white shirt that a now dead Felipe was wearing. He kept wiping until the knife was clean. "That is what happens when you are disloyal. It will not be tolerated...ever." Alejo made direct contact with each of his family member at the round table then focused on Allen. "I want to personally apologize to you and your sons. I do not condone what Felipe and Hector did and they have now paid the price with their lives."

"Apology accepted," Allen said.

"Yeah, now lets get the fuck outta here," Clayton whispered to his father as the three men stood in unison not speaking another word until they were out the building.

"What type of shit was that?" Kasir mumbled.

"I told you that old man was fuckin' crazy," Clayton said shaking his head as they got into their waiting SUV.

"I think we all knew he was crazy just not that

crazy. Alejo know he could've slit them boys throats after we left," Allen huffed. "He just wanted us to see the fuckin' blood too and ruin our afternoon," he added before chuckling.

"I think it was more than just that," Clayton replied, looking out the tinted window as the driver pulled out the parking lot.

"Then what?" Kasir questioned.

"I think old man Alejo was trying to make a point, not only to his family members but to us too."

"You might be right, Clayton."

"I know I'm right. We need to keep all eyes on Alejo 'cause I don't trust him. He might've killed his crooked ass nephews to show good faith but trust me that man hates to ever be wrong about anything. What he did to those nephews is probably what he really wanted to do to us but he knew nobody would've left that building alive. The only truth Alejo spoke in there was that he was raised by wolves," Clayton scoffed leaning back in the car seat.

All three men remained silent for the duration of the drive. Each pondering what had transpired in what was supposed to be a simple business meeting that turned into a double homicide. They also thought about the point Clayton said Alejo was trying to make. No one wanted that to be true as their business with the Alejo family was a lucrative one for everyone involved. But for men like Alejo, sometimes pride held more value than the almighty dollar, which made him extremely dangerous.

P.O. Box 912
Collierville, TN 38027

www.joydejaking.com
www.twitter.com/joydejaking

A King Production

QUANTITY	TITLES	PRICE	TOTAL
	Bitch	$15.00	
	Bitch Reloaded	$15.00	
	The Bitch Is Back	$15.00	
	Queen Bitch	$15.00	
	Last Bitch Standing	$15.00	
	Superstar	$15.00	
	Ride Wit' Me	$12.00	
	Ride Wit' Me Part 2	$15.00	
	Stackin' Paper	$15.00	
	Trife Life To Lavish	$15.00	
	Trife Life To Lavish II	$15.00	
	Stackin' Paper II	$15.00	
	Rich or Famous	$15.00	
	Rich or Famous Part 2	$15.00	
	Rich or Famous Part 3	$15.00	
	Bitch A New Beginning	$15.00	
	Mafia Princess Part 1	$15.00	
	Mafia Princess Part 2	$15.00	
	Mafia Princess Part 3	$15.00	
	Mafia Princess Part 4	$15.00	
	Mafia Princess Part 5	$15.00	
	Boss Bitch	$15.00	
	Baller Bitches Vol. 1	$15.00	
	Baller Bitches Vol. 2	$15.00	
	Baller Bitches Vol. 3	$15.00	
	Bad Bitch	$15.00	
	Still The Baddest Bitch	$15.00	
	Power	$15.00	
	Power Part 2	$15.00	
	Drake	$15.00	
	Drake Part 2	$15.00	
	Female Hustler	$15.00	
	Female Hustler Part 2	$15.00	
	Princess Fever "Birthday Bash"	$9.99	
	Nico Carter The Men Of The Bitch Series	$15.00	
	Bitch The Beginning Of The End	$15.00	
	Supreme...Men Of The Bitch Series	$15.00	
	Coke Like The 80s	$15.00	
	Bitch The Final Chapter	$15.00	

Shipping/Handling (Via Priority Mail) $6.50 1-2 Books, $8.95 3-4 Books add $1.95 for ea. Additional book.

Total: $_____ FORMS OF ACCEPTED PAYMENTS: Certified or government issued checks and money Orders, all mail in orders take 5-7 Business days to be delivered